HEARTSIDE BAY

Never a Perfect Moment

CATHY COLE

■SCHOLASTIC

Scholastic Children's Books
An imprint of Scholastic Ltd
Euston House, 24 Eversholt Street, London, NW1 1DB, UK
Registered office: Westfield Road, Southam, Warwickshire, CV47 0RA
SCHOLASTIC and associated logos are trademarks and/or
registered trademarks of Scholastic Inc.

First published in the UK by Scholastic Ltd, 2014

Text copyright © Scholastic Ltd, 2014

ISBN 978 1407 14050 6

Falkirk Council	
Askews & Holts	2014
JF T	£6.99

13 5 7 9 10 8 6 4 2

This is a work of fiction. Names, characters, places, incidents
and dialogues are products of the author's imagination or are used
fictitiously. Any resemblance to actual people, living or dead,
events or locales is entirely coincidental.

www.scholastic.co.uk

Hugs and kisses to Lucy Courtenay
and Sara Grant

ONE

The noise in the school canteen dimmed to nothing as Polly Nelson stared at the text. Her palms felt clammy, like the phone was about to slip from her hands. She couldn't quite believe what her eyes were telling her. But there it was, as plain as day.

Dinner Fri?

The text blurred. Now all she could see was the name that went with it, highlighted across the top of her phone screen.

Ollie Wright.

Ollie Wright was asking her out on a date!

OK, so the text wasn't exactly romantic. In fact, it

was pretty basic. The sentimental side of Polly was a little disappointed. Who asked a girl out with just two words? There weren't even any kisses at the bottom.

She scolded herself almost immediately. Why exactly did that matter? This was *Ollie* they were talking about. The school's best-looking football star and most popular boy at Heartside High. Asking her, quirky, shy Polly Nelson, out on a date.

You're allowed to be excited, she thought. She'd wanted this for so long. She'd been in love with Ollie for years. A lifetime. In some ways it didn't make sense – they were so different. But she couldn't help it.

She glanced up from her phone, to see if she could spot Ollie in the crowded canteen. Everyone was wearing black armbands and matching sombre expressions. The hall was full of the usual clattering of crockery and cutlery, but the lunchtime chatter was missing. Hardly anyone was talking, and if they were, they were almost whispering, glancing around as if they were breaking some unspoken rule.

Oh Ollie, Polly thought unhappily. *Your timing sucks.*

Ryan Jameson's fatal cliff jump hung over them

2

all like a heavy shroud. It had been less than a week since his funeral, and his death had changed the whole atmosphere at Heartside High. The corridors had been quiet for days, and the usual press around the lockers between classes was silent and awkward, just like here in the canteen. Feeling excited about anything just felt – wrong. What gave Polly the right to feel something that Ryan would never feel again?

Polly studied Ollie's text again as she let her hair swing around her face. She had dyed it black to match her mood, and the dark strands contrasted sharply with her pale, clear skin and light hazel eyes. She wasn't sure the colour suited her, but she couldn't muster the energy to care.

Was it wrong to think about going on a date? She felt sad and guilty and giddy, all at the same time.

Ollie was totally wrong for her. She'd always known that. Apart from being way out of her league looks-wise, Ollie shared none of Polly's interests. Art meant nothing to him. Literature, fashion, animal rights – nothing. All he cared about was playing football and having fun. He was extremely good at both. Polly couldn't stand most of the boys on the football team. She didn't understand how they could care so much about football, which was so boring and meaningless to her.

Opposites attracted, Polly had heard that before. But did they last? Would she and Ollie ever really work together? How could they when they had precisely nothing in common? *And* Ollie had just broken up with Polly's best friend, Lila. This would have normally broken the number-one rule of friendship, but Lila had given Polly and Ollie her blessing to go out with each other.

"You and Ollie must grab all the happiness you can," Lila had said after Ryan's death. It still felt wrong, though.

Polly looked across the table to where Lila was staring silently out of the window. Lila had been particularly affected by Ryan's death, and had said very little for days. Everyone knew Ryan had jumped off that cliff to impress her. It was a heavy burden to bear and Polly knew that Lila felt it intensely.

It was a relief to think about someone else's problems, Polly realized. It was much easier wondering how to cheer Lila up than how to bridge the obvious gap between her and Ollie.

Lila needs someone to take her mind off Ryan, she thought. Plus, if Lila was interested in someone else, it would make Polly feel less guilty about Ollie. Lila's eyes had a particular sparkle about them when she was interested in a boy. It was a sparkle Polly hadn't seen very often in the last week. The only time she had noticed it, Polly realized, was when Lila was talking to Josh Taylor.

Anyone with half a brain could see that Josh was crazy about Lila. There was a kind of electricity in the air when they were together. Lila may not have been able to see it, but they were meant for each other. All it would take to get them together was a little nudge.

"Lila?"

Lila looked at Polly with faraway eyes. "What?"

Polly realized how crass it would sound to voice her thoughts out loud. *Why don't you go out with Josh and forget about Ryan? He may be dead, but you're still alive!*

"I . . . forgot what I was going to say," she said. "It was nothing important. Sorry."

Lila stood up and shouldered her bag. "See you in class," she said, and trudged away.

5

Polly watched her friend until she had left the dinner hall. Absently, she looked back at her text. Ollie would be waiting for a reply. What should she say?

She glanced around again, wondering if Ollie was somewhere in the crowd. It felt like there were more people in here than usual.

Like a wave retreating from the beach, the crowd seemed to part. Several girls nudged each other. Ollie was striding towards Polly, blond hair tousled, a smile on his face. That old familiar feeling zipped through Polly's body at the sight of him: his happy face, his blue eyes. It happened every time she saw him. She couldn't help it. It was chemistry, pure and simple.

Ollie reached Polly's table. He smiled down at her. "Hey," he said. "You ever going to answer my text?"

Polly felt herself melting. *Be cool*, she thought, struggling not to fall straight into his arms.

"I'm . . . thinking about it," she said.

Ollie pulled a mock-sad face. Digging around in his pocket, he produced a little dark-red box which he held out to her.

Polly stared at the box. "What's that?"

"A little something," he said. "In case you need persuading."

He placed the little box in her palm. Polly's skin fizzed at the touch of his hand. She opened the box slowly.

Nestled in the creamy satin lining was a gorgeous vintage locket on a slim silver chain. Engraved in the middle of the locket were the initials "PN".

"They're my initials," Polly said, staring at the locket in wonder.

"I got one thing right then," Ollie said. He sounded nervous. "Aren't you going to open it?"

Polly's heart was thumping so loudly she couldn't hear herself think. She slid her thumbnail between the two halves of the locket and gave a gentle flick. It opened like a clamshell, revealing a tiny photograph pressed inside. A photo of her and Ollie, together.

"I've wanted to go out with you for ages, Polly," said Ollie quietly. "Say yes."

He touched her cheek with one finger and walked away, disappearing into the crowd again.

Polly gazed at the locket. Her heart felt full to overflowing. Now *that* was the perfect way to ask for a first date.

Her fingers felt clumsy as she fastened the locket around her neck, tucking the silver case down inside her shirt. She took out her phone, stared one more time at the little two-word message.

There was only one possible answer.

TWO

The locket felt cool and heavy against Polly's skin. Ollie really liked her. He'd liked her for as long as she'd liked him. Her heart swelled to bursting. Three little letters and one big exclamation mark was all that stood between her and the thing she had wanted for so long. She knew exactly what she was going to reply.

Yes!

She hit send.

There was a whoop from somewhere down the dining hall. Ollie was on his feet, holding his arms in the air.

"I'm going out with a beautiful girl on Friday!" he cried.

His joy clashed horribly with the atmosphere in the dining hall. Polly blushed furiously but giggled at the disapproving faces turned in Ollie's direction. She couldn't help the way she felt.

Ryan would understand, she thought.

She hugged her phone to her chest. It had been so long since she had last smiled. It was a good feeling.

The sound system crackled over the dining-hall speakers.

"Would Lila Murray, Josh Taylor and Polly Nelson please go the office?"

Polly felt the smile drop off her face like a stone. She was wanted in the office? That was only ever bad news. What had she done?

She looked around for Lila, before remembering her friend had already left the dining hall. Josh was nowhere to be seen. She hoped he wasn't down by the beach, sketching, the way he often did during lunch break.

Polly quickly left the dining hall and headed towards the head teacher's office. Why were she, Lila and Josh being summoned like this? She hoped they weren't in trouble. There had been so much trouble lately, she wasn't sure she could take much more.

Josh's familiar loping stride was some way ahead of her along the corridor. Polly broke into a nervous run.

"Hey, Josh," she panted, catching him up. "What do you think this is about?"

Josh glanced at her over the top of his glasses. "We haven't broken into any shopping centres in the middle of the night recently, have we?"

Polly gulped as she remembered their unauthorized trip to Eve's dad's half-built shopping centre. They had just managed to avoid getting caught by some security guards.

Lila was waiting by the head teacher's office already, her face tight with strain. Her eyes lit up at the sight of Josh and Polly.

"What's going on?" she said at once. "What have we done?"

"I've done nothing, I swear," said Josh. "Apart from draw a very unflattering picture of Mr Cartwright which made him look like a stoat. And I'm pretty sure he doesn't know about that."

Lila laughed, her eyes sparkling like in the old days. Polly wondered when her friend would wake up to the fact that Josh was the perfect boy for her.

Mr Cartwright's secretary, Miss Oliphant, opened the door. "In here," she said briskly. "Chief Murray is waiting."

Polly's heart sped up. Josh looked pale.

"What's my *dad* doing here?" Lila said with an audible gasp.

"His job, I imagine," said Miss Oliphant, pursing her lips. "Come along."

Chief Murray looked a lot like Lila, Polly thought. Same brown hair, same bright blue eyes. He beckoned them into the small meeting room beside Miss Oliphant's desk. Mr Cartwright stood by the door with his hands behind his back.

Lila slumped warily in the chair furthest away from her dad. Josh sat beside Polly.

"What's that?" said Polly nervously, pointing at the small black device in the middle of the table.

"We're recording this interview," said Chief Murray. "There's nothing to worry about. It's not official. Just pretend it isn't there."

Polly felt panicky. The room felt small and airless. The recording device crouched on the table like a black toad.

"I have a few more questions about Ryan Jameson's death," said Chief Murray, flicking through a brown folder on the table.

"We have classes this afternoon," Lila said sullenly, shifting in her chair.

"I have assured Mr Cartwright that this won't take long," said Chief Murray. "I would like you to go over something one more time. Where were you all when Ryan jumped from the cliff?"

"We've answered that already," said Lila. Her voice was trembling. "On the night it happened. At the police station. How many more times do we have to answer stupid questions like this?"

"There is nothing stupid about a boy's death, Lila," said Chief Murray sharply.

Lila bit her lip and fell silent.

Polly was taking deep breaths. Her heart rate was all over the place, and she could feel her vision narrowing and tightening.

"I was on the beach." Her voice sounded strange

to her own ears. "I wasn't on the clifftop when Ryan jumped."

Chief Murray checked his notes and added a scribble in the margin of a page headed POLLY NELSON. Polly squeezed her fists together tightly. *Breathe*, she told herself. *In and out. In and out. Easy.*

"Josh?" asked Chief Murray, glancing up.

Josh looked paler than ever. "I was on the cliff. I jumped into the water after Ryan when he didn't come up. But I was. . ."

Josh trailed off. He didn't need to say it. *Too late.*

"And can you remember any of the conversation leading up to Ryan making that fatal jump?" said Chief Murray.

"We've said all this, over and over," Lila hissed. "Ryan was boasting that he could make the jump. We tried to stop him. He didn't listen."

Chief Murray looked at another sheet of paper. Polly could see that it had Lila's name on it. "And you were with Ryan on the cliff as well, Lila?"

Lila was growing paler and more agitated by the minute. "You *know* I was. Why do we have to keep going over this? You know I don't like thinking about that night, Dad. Why are you doing this to me?"

Polly reached for Lila's hand, sensing her friend's fear and regret. "It wasn't your fault, you know," she said. "There was nothing any of us could do to stop Ryan."

Lila pulled her hand away. She folded her arms tightly across her body. "Ryan's parents don't see it that way," she said bitterly.

"Are there many more questions, Chief Murray?" asked Josh.

Chief Murray steepled his fingers. "I wanted to ask about Eve Somerstown."

Polly blinked. "What do you want to know?" she asked in surprise.

"Anything you can tell me." Chief Murray's expression was intent, his eyes trained on them like blue searchlights. "Her family life. Her father and his finances."

"What's that got to do with Ryan's death? Why do you have to know everyone's business?" Lila spat.

"I'll ask the questions," Chief Murray responded sternly.

Polly tried to claw the conversation back to a less aggressive level. "Eve's rich and . . . can be difficult," she said, carefully. She didn't particularly trust Eve, but she didn't want to gossip about her either. She was going through a tough time at the moment. "Her dad's the mayor. He has lots of successful businesses. But you know that right?"

"That party must have cost a fortune," Chief Murray commented. "Did her father pay for it? Your trip to the shopping centre – what did you see there?"

Polly blanched. He knew about their midnight adventure in Mr Somerstown's half-built shopping complex?

"There's no point denying that you were there the other night," said Chief Murray, catching Polly's expression and reading it correctly. "You're lucky you haven't been charged for trespassing. What do you think's going on there?"

Josh spread his hands. "It's a shopping centre," he said. "One day, it'll be full of shops."

"Hmm," said Chief Murray.

Lila pushed her chair back violently. "I'm sick of these questions. I want to go to class."

Mr Cartwright started forward with his hands raised. "Lila, I'm sure your father has nearly—"

"Your questions are embarrassing and pointless," Lila snarled at her dad. Tears glinted on her cheeks. "Eve's business is her own. I'm out of here."

She stormed out of the room, slamming the door so hard that it juddered on its hinges.

Chief Murray rubbed his hands through his hair. Polly thought he looked tired. "Thank you for your time, Polly, Josh. Mr Cartwright," he said. "I'll see myself out."

It was a relief to be out of that little room with its whirring tape recorder. Polly felt lighter the moment they shut the office door behind them.

"She's not handing this well, is she?" Josh remarked.

There was no need to ask who he meant.

Polly felt herself relaxing again in the role of helping her friends. "You know, Josh," she said as they headed to their classes, "you should ask Lila out."

Josh stopped dead. "What?"

"You should," Polly insisted.

Josh pushed his glasses up his nose. "I tried once,"

he admitted. "It didn't work out quite the way I intended. She obviously doesn't like me in that way."

Boys knew nothing, Polly thought.

"Maybe she didn't once," she said. "But she does now. Believe me, Josh. Girls know this stuff."

Colour was stealing across Josh's pale cheeks. "You think?"

Polly thought of Lila's miserable face. Of Ryan, lying face down in the water on that terrible night.

"What have you got to lose?" she said. "Life is meant to be lived, right?"

Josh stopped by the staffroom. "I'm going this way," he said, thumbing over his shoulder. "See you later, OK?"

"Are you going to ask her?" Polly pressed.

"I'll think about it," he said with a little smile.

Polly smiled back, feeling pleased. "Don't leave it too long, will you? We all need to start having a little more fun around here," she said, thinking of Ollie.

THREE

Polly was so deep in thought that she almost bumped into Rhi in the corridor.

Rhi looked drained and there were visible circles beneath her eyes. Her hair, which usually framed her face in a dark and curly cloud, had been pulled back and secured with grips, as if leaving it loose would express unforgivable light-heartedness in the face of tragedy. She was still one of the prettiest girls in school, Polly reflected. Polly touched her own hair self-consciously, thinking again that it was a mistake to dye it black.

Rhi's expressive dark eyes were bright, and more curious than Polly had seen them in days. "What did Mr Cartwright want with you guys? Everyone's been speculating like mad. Are you in trouble?"

"Lila's dad was here and just wanted to ask more questions about Ryan."

"I thought they'd asked all the questions by now," said Rhi in surprise.

"You'd think so, wouldn't you?" Polly said. "I guess they're tying up loose ends and trying to close the case. I'm sure the whole family needs closure on this. It must be awful."

Rhi's eyes looked as if they were reddening again.

"I know it's awful of me, but I'm so *sick* of the gloom," Polly sighed, leaning back against the lockers. "We all need a night out at the Heartbeat or somewhere. It's been ages since we met up and had any fun. Are you busy tonight?"

Rhi looked at her strangely. "The Heartbeat Café's still closed, Polly. Ryan's whole family is in mourning. Besides, I don't think we're ready for it yet. It would feel too weird without Ryan there."

Polly wanted to kick herself. How could she have been so insensitive? "Of course," she said awkwardly. "Stupid of me. It's just . . . I want all this to go away, you know? Get back to normal."

Rhi looked at her hands. "When we lost my

sister in the car crash, I wanted everything to go back to normal too," she said quietly. "But it never did. When someone dies, nothing is the same, ever again."

Tears spilled down Rhi's cheeks. Polly was appalled at herself. She'd put her foot in it twice, in as many seconds. That had to be some kind of record.

"Rhi, I'm so sorry," she said helplessly. "Can you forgive me for talking without thinking?"

Rhi rubbed the tears from her face. "It's not you. I feel like a leaky tap at the moment," she said with a shaky laugh. "This whole thing with Ryan has brought back some really tough memories. And not just for me. For my parents as well."

Polly touched Rhi's arm in sympathy. "Is it really bad at home?"

"Pretty bad, yeah," Rhi admitted. "Dad's been spending time with Mr Jameson, helping him work through his grief. Maybe it's helpful, being with someone who understands what it feels like to lose a child. But Dad's coming home with all this extra grief on his shoulders. It's hard to be around him just now. Mum's not talking about it, but you can see on her face how much it's affected her. She's working even harder than she usually does, trying to pretend that everything's OK."

"That must be so difficult."

Polly could hardly imagine what Rhi and her parents were going through. She found a tissue in her pocket and handed it over. Rhi took it gratefully.

"Everything's such a mess," she sniffed into the tissue. "I wish I could rewind it all."

Polly knew exactly what Rhi meant. "None of this was your fault," she reminded her friend.

"Wasn't it?" Rhi's eyes were haunted. "You weren't even up on the cliff when it happened, Polly. It was surreal. One minute we were all singing along to one of Brody's songs and the firelight was flickering over the rocks – and then Ryan and Lila appeared and everything changed."

"Don't go through it all again, Rhi—"

"I have to," Rhi interrupted. "I have to work out if I could have prevented it, you know? Max told Ryan not to jump. Ryan called him a chicken. I was sitting *right there*. I could have grabbed Ryan, maybe, or. . ."

"Please don't, Rhi," said Polly helplessly. "You can't change any of it. It was an accident."

A bell rang somewhere overhead, signifying the start of afternoon classes. Rhi blew her nose and struggled to compose herself. Polly could hardly bear to see the misery on her friend's face. She had to make Rhi smile again.

"So the Heartbeat Café was one of my dumber ideas," she said. "But I still think we should get together. Just the girls, maybe. You could all come over to my house. It would be good to talk, don't you think? Properly. Not just for five minutes, snatched between school bells. We haven't all been together since the day of Ryan's funeral. That afternoon on the beach."

Polly could picture that day so clearly in her mind. She and Rhi, crossing the wind-blown beach to where Lila and Eve were standing beside the pretty memorial they had made for Ryan in the sand. Eve, telling them all that she was gay.

"When you say 'the girls'," said Rhi, interrupting Polly's train of thought, "does that include Eve?"

"Yes," said Polly. "We vowed on the beach that day that we would try and be better friends for each other, didn't we? And although she's a difficult person to be friends with, that means Eve too."

Rhi looked unhappy. "I'm not ready to spend time with Eve yet."

Polly frowned. "Why not? Because she's gay?"

"No, of course not. I don't have a problem with that," said Rhi, shaking her head. "It's her *lies*. They've destroyed any feelings of friendship I used to have for her. She stole Max from me, Polly. She broke my heart. And then the next minute she says she's gay! How can someone do that? Wreck a person's life by taking their boyfriend, when they don't even like boys? Why did she do it? Just to hurt me? Just to prove she could?"

"It doesn't make much sense," Polly agreed. "But Eve's never followed the rules, has she? She'll be hurting over Ryan, just like we are. She needs us too."

Rhi sighed and started walking towards the classroom. "Are you coming or not?"

More students were pouring through the corridors now, making their way to afternoon classes. Polly dodged through the crowd, trying to catch up with Rhi.

"How are things with you and Max anyway?"

Rhi teetered her hand from side to side. "We're sort of dating again."

"That's what you want," Polly said. "Isn't it?"

"I don't know," Rhi said with a shrug. "He wants to pick up where we left off, like the whole thing with Eve never happened. Like it didn't matter. But I'm not so sure. The whole business with Ryan has reminded me that we only have one life, you know? Lila keeps telling me I can do better than Max." She looked at Polly questioningly. "What do you think?"

Polly had never much liked Max. He was too . . . *charming* was the word she wanted. Like all he had to do was smile and the world would fall into place, just the way he wanted it to. He'd so easily cheated on Rhi with Eve, and then just as easily persuaded Rhi to take him back. It was like there were no consequences for him, like he didn't even feel any guilt about what he'd done.

"It doesn't matter what I think," she said diplomatically. "I'm not the one going out with him. But you can't avoid the fact that he cheated on you, Rhi. Who's to say he won't do it again?"

Rhi rubbed her hands through her hair. "I've dated

him for so long," she sighed. "We have all these shared memories, and he knows me so well. What if he's the one, Polly? How do you know if the risk is worth it?"

"That," said Polly, "is an excellent question."

And I wish I knew the answer, she thought.

FOUR

Polly didn't have a good night. The gloom at school hung over her like a cloud, and she found it almost impossible to think all the peaceful, calming things she needed to think about in order to fall asleep. She'd tried everything – having a bath, drinking hot chocolate, spraying her pillow with lavender mist. But every time she got close to drifting off, Josh's horrified cry on discovering Ryan's body came into her mind, a piercing howl of horror that brought her out in a cold sweat. The situation with Ollie didn't help either. The more she thought about it, the more she felt anxious about their date on Friday. She had liked him for so long, but they were so different – physically *and* mentally. How would it ever work?

Morning took a long time to arrive. Polly found herself getting up early, having breakfast before her mum was awake, and taking herself down the hill to school with almost half an hour to spare.

She texted Eve and Lila as she walked.

Everything OK? Worried about you.

As she tapped send, she wondered uneasily if she'd hear from either of them before she saw them in class. She'd phoned them both the night before, and again before breakfast. Her calls had gone to voicemail. Four texts later and she still hadn't had a reply. It was very unlike them both to leave a message unanswered. She didn't like to think about what might have happened. Polly couldn't help imagining worst-case scenarios, and tried not to let herself do it any more often than she had to. It was too disturbing.

Pocketing her phone with a sigh, Polly switched her bag to her other shoulder. The wind seemed determined to blow her skirt over her head this morning. The coats of her fellow pedestrians billowed around them like the sails on the ships out in Heartside harbour. Clouds scudded through the sky, racing each other towards the cliffs that surrounded the bay.

At the newsagent's on the corner, Polly paused, checking the traffic. Looking to her right, her eye was caught by three brightly coloured pictures on the front of the *Heartside Herald*, flapping over its usual rail outside the newsagent's door.

It took a moment to register what she was seeing.

Chief Murray looked harassed in his photo as he stepped out of the Heartside police station, flanked by two officers in uniform. In the facing picture, Eve's father held up his hand to ward off the flashing bulbs of the photographers. The picture in the centre was a picture Polly had come to know well: Ryan, smart in school uniform and smiling through his overlong fringe at the world.

ACCIDENTAL DEATH?
Following the tragic death of Ryan Jameson (15) of Heartside Bay ten days ago in a cliff-jumping incident, Chief of Police Greg Murray issued the following statement: "Ryan Jameson's death was a tragic accident that has cut out the heart of our

community. We are united in our grief, and our condolences are extended to Ryan's family."

The official verdict may be accidental death, but the *Heartside Herald* can reveal a very different side of the story. Our reporter was granted an exclusive interview yesterday with Ryan's mother, Mrs Louise Jameson (42). He met with her in her cosily furnished apartment above the Jamesons' family business, well-known local establishment the Heartbeat Café.

Mrs Jameson, bearing up bravely under the weight of her terrible grief, issued the following statement: "Heartside Bay is a divided community, whatever Chief Murray says. There are the haves and the have-nots. We aren't a wealthy family. Ryan suffered the consequences of this at school, where he was routinely excluded and teased for not fitting in. It was the reckless behaviour of Heartside Bay's wilder, more privileged teenagers that drove Ryan to his death – among them, Chief Murray's own daughter. What does that say about our so-called community?

"Mayor Henry Somerstown, whose daughter

held the extravagant, fatally unsupervised party on one of the uninhabited islands off the coast, has Ryan's blood on his hands. I hope he can sleep at night. As a family, we will never sleep again."

Food for thought, readers. Are we a divided community, as Mrs Jameson alleges? How much longer can we allow our more privileged sector of youngsters to wreck lives in this way?

The words swam before Polly's eyes. Although she felt huge sympathy for Ryan's mother, she also felt sick with disbelief at the injustice of what she was reading. She didn't want to think ill of the dead, but the fact remained: *Ryan* had been the reckless one. They had warned him not to jump. No one had pushed him. No one had encouraged him. But he had jumped anyway.

The world's gone crazy, Polly thought numbly.

She had been standing for several moments on the street corner, gazing at the newspaper, when her phone buzzed in her pocket. She pulled it out and stared at the screen.

Ollie was calling.

A flash of happiness ran through her. She savoured the sight of his name on her phone before a stab of guilt hit her. She shoved her phone back into her pocket, unanswered. She had no right to feel happy. Not with Ryan dead, a family destroyed and a newspaper telling lies about her friends.

She shivered to think how Lila and Eve must be feeling today. The newspaper explained why they hadn't answered their phones. They'd probably known the story was going to be printed.

Her phone was still vibrating in her pocket. Polly gritted her teeth. She couldn't answer it. She felt too guilty. Too nervous, if she was honest. Ollie would have to wait.

She couldn't go to school straight away. She needed air, and time to think. Changing direction, she shouldered her bag more securely and hurried across the street, her black hair swinging about her face, and headed for the beach.

The wide swing of sand was empty this morning, the gulls having difficulty flying in a straight line. Polly's skirt snapped about her legs like a whip. Reaching the water's edge, she stood square on to the wind, letting it rip through her. Willing it to snatch away all the confusion and chaos of her life.

The sight of the sea always calmed her. She'd spent hours down here after her parents' divorce, when she and her mum had first moved to Heartside from California. Sitting on the sea wall and watching the tide felt familiar at a time when everything was changing. And she had spent time by the water after her break-up with her first boyfriend, Sam. Polly had to smile as she remembered the way they had met. The beach had played an important part in that as well. It seemed like ages ago, though. So much had happened since then. Getting to know Lila. The shock of learning her mother was gay and dating Polly's history teacher, Ms Andrews. Then Ryan's death. And now Ollie.

When did life get so complicated? Will it ever be simple again? she wondered hopelessly.

Maybe it never would.

Wherever Ryan was now, at least he didn't have to deal with life and its endless problems any more. In that respect, he was lucky. She shivered as she realized she didn't really mean that at all.

"Polly?"

Polly froze. For the weirdest couple of seconds, she wondered if Ryan's ghost was calling her across the waves.

Someone grabbed her around the waist and pulled her into a tight embrace. Polly opened her mouth and let out a piercing scream, making the gulls above her head take fright and wheel away over the sea.

FIVE

"Hey," Ollie said in surprise, grappling with Polly as she flailed at him with her fists, shielding his face from her blows. "It's me! What's the matter? Why are you hitting me?"

Polly stopped screaming abruptly as her face flushed bright scarlet. Ollie was the last person she had expected to see.

He was so tall and handsome. The wind had brightened his cheeks and made his eyes sparkle. Standing beside him, Polly felt like a very small and ugly crab.

"Ollie?" she stammered. She could hardly bring herself to look at him. "What are you doing here?"

"I was worried about you when you didn't answer

your phone. You're not going to hit me again," he said cautiously, "are you?"

"Of course not, I thought. . ."

Polly trailed off. What had she thought? That Ryan had come back from the dead and tried to drag her into the sea to join him? She really was cracking up.

"What?" Ollie asked, looking curious.

"Nothing," said Polly, embarrassed. "Sorry I didn't answer the phone. I was . . . thinking."

"Sounds dangerous," Ollie joked.

Polly sighed inwardly. She knew he was joking, but sometimes she just wasn't in the mood. She wanted someone who she could discuss her problems and thoughts with, but it didn't seem like Ollie would ever be interested in that. He was so flippant about everything. That was the problem with Ollie and her. Right there, in a nutshell. Sure, her pulse raced when she looked into his eyes, but every conversation they had made her question whether they had enough in common to ever really work together.

Ollie huddled into his coat. The wind was

doing crazy things to his hair. "You saw the paper, right?"

So Ollie had seen it too. Polly nodded. "It's awful. And completely untrue."

"Not to Mrs Jameson." Ollie looked sad. "She must really be suffering. It's clear that she hates us all."

Ollie might not think much, but Polly knew his heart was in the right place. His arms were still round her. However hard she tried to reason herself out of this, she couldn't help the fluttery feeling in her stomach at the warmth of him – the boy she'd had a crush on for such a long time.

"Anyway," Ollie went on, "when you didn't answer your phone I guessed you might be on the beach. So I came to find you. And here I am."

"How did you guess I'd be on the beach?"

"I know you, Polly," he said simply.

Polly desperately wanted to pour her heart out to him. All her awful anxieties, and the way she wasn't sleeping well, and her fears for her friends. The way the memory of Ryan haunted her. But she'd never talked to Ollie about stuff like that before. Normally they flirted, and teased, and wound each other up. She'd mock him for some stupid remark he'd made; he'd poke fun at the latest vintage outfit that she'd customized. Proper feelings and raw emotions? They were a different territory altogether. They were terrifying. And she wasn't sure he'd like the real her.

He brushed her cheek. "OK?"

Polly couldn't bring herself to say anything. She hugged him instead, and enjoyed the strength of his chest and arms as he hugged her right back. Maybe there was more to Ollie than just a pretty face and fit body. Would she allow herself to find out?

"Thanks for coming to find me," she said, looking up at him shyly. "I was feeling very alone."

"You're not alone any more," he said.

They walked off the beach hand in hand, heading for school. Ollie's palm was warm and comforting, his fingers curled protectively around her own. The melting feeling in her stomach was threatening to take over. She wished he would kiss her. She desperately hoped he wouldn't. She was such a mess.

"Still on for our date tomorrow?" he said, glancing at her.

Polly's stomach flip-flopped. She had put the locket on again this morning. She could feel it nestling against her skin, beneath her shirt. "Can't wait," she said honestly.

"I have a few surprises up my sleeve," he said, waggling his eyebrows.

Polly felt nervous. "What kind of surprises?"

"Oh, you'll love them. There's skydiving, and the swimming with crocodiles . . ."

There was a teasing glint in Ollie's blue eyes that made Polly's cheek's flush.

". . . and the little toy at the bottom of the Happy Meal. . ." she teased back.

"I would never take my girlfriend to McDonald's," Ollie said, mock offended.

Girlfriend. The word made Polly squirm with pleasure. Was she Ollie's girlfriend? In what universe was this magic allowed to happen?

"KFC, on the other hand?" he went on. "*Now* we're talking."

Polly giggled. She felt so . . . *free.* It felt right. She felt happy.

As if someone had flipped a switch, they stopped

laughing the moment they arrived at school. The school flag was hanging at half-mast, flapping sadly in the wind. People were mounting the steps, arms wrapped around school bags and heads down. No one was talking, let alone laughing.

Ollie's hand suddenly felt strange in Polly's, like it wasn't supposed to be there. It was as if the school had the power to drain all her happiness away. She tried to pull her hand away, feeling crushed with guilt all of a sudden. Ollie held on firmly.

"Don't," he said, looking into her eyes. "Please."

Polly reluctantly left her hand where it was. "It feels wrong," she said, biting her lip.

"Wrong to be doing something Ryan will never do again?" said Ollie.

Polly flinched. That was it exactly. "Yes," she whispered.

Ollie held her hand even more tightly. "We can't stop living because Ryan is dead, Polly. If anything, we should live *more*. We should live every single second of our lives to the full, because you never know what might happen next."

It was strange, hearing Ollie talk so seriously.

"So you're a philosopher now?" Polly said. It was the only response she could think of.

Ollie slid his arms slowly around her waist. "I'm deadly serious. We have to live for the moment, Polly. It's what it's all about."

He was pulling her closer. Polly felt scared and excited. Were they about to kiss?

"Hey, lovebirds," said Max, breezily barging between them. "Have you heard about Eve?"

Polly felt angry and annoyed as Max winked at her and punched Ollie on the arm. How dare he barge in like that? Couldn't he see that she and Ollie were about to — ? He was *so* not the right person for lovely, gentle, sensitive Rhi.

"Max, mate, you pick your moments," said Ollie, rubbing his arm.

"So have you?" Max asked, unfazed. "Heard about Eve?"

"Of course we have," Polly snapped, reeling from a combination of shock and disappointment. "The whole world probably knows by now. Ryan's mother blames Eve's dad, irresponsible parenting, rich kids gone wild, the *Heartside Herald*, blah blah blah. As I recall, you enjoyed that party just as much as the rest of us! Can't we put all the bad feeling about Ryan's death behind us yet?"

"Not that," said Max. His eyes gleamed. "Did you hear Eve is gay?"

SIX

"No way," said Ollie in surprise.

"That's what I said," Max replied, nodding vigorously. "But everyone's talking about it. Do you think it's true?"

Polly wanted to slap Max's stupid grinning face. Eve was gay. So what? Polly's mother was gay too. Big sparkly deal.

"I mean," Max continued as they went up the steps into school together, "she can't be gay. I *dated* her."

Like dating you would make it impossible for a girl to like another girl? Polly thought with disgust. Max knew nothing about the human heart, that much was clear.

Max poked Ollie in the ribs. "You dated her too."

43

"I never dated Eve," protested Ollie. "It would have been like dating a snake. I wouldn't have known when she was going to bite me."

"Dated, kissed, whatever. You have had *lip knowledge* of Eve Somerstown, Ollie. Don't deny it."

Ollie flushed. "Leave it, will you Max?"

Polly was feeling increasingly weird about this conversation. She was pretty sure Ollie had never kissed Eve, but what did she know? Eve had liked Ollie for ages before he started dating Lila. The thought of Ollie and Eve together made her feel a little sick.

"Maybe she kissed you and then went off the idea of guys all together," Max laughed. "Your technique must really suck, Ollie. Imagine! Eve! A lesbian!"

Polly had heard enough. "If it's such a crazy idea," she blurted out, "how come we're still talking about it?"

"Because it's juicy gossip," said Max, rubbing his hands. "And everyone loves gossip, don't they?"

"Where did you hear this rumour anyway?" Ollie demanded.

Max pointed at Polly. "She's not denying it, I see," he grinned.

44

"It's nothing to do with me," Polly muttered. She didn't want to be the one to "out" Eve at school.

Max's eyes shone with interest. "Has Eve tried it on with you, then?"

"You're so predictable, Max," Polly said, moved to anger. How did anyone in this school find Max cool and interesting? He was clever, sure. But there was a slickness about him that made Polly think of oil spreading over clear blue water. "Eve's sexuality is her own business, OK?"

"Your silence says it all!" Max crowed. "It must be true!"

"Seriously, Max," Ollie pressed, "where did you hear this?"

Max winked. "Around. See you."

He loped off with his hands in his pockets.

Ollie whistled. "That's some rumour. Has Eve talked to you about this, Polly? I can't believe she might be gay."

"Does it really matter if she is?" said Polly angrily. "Seriously? This is the twenty-first century, Ollie."

She dropped his hand. "I've got to get to class."

Polly stormed away down the corridor. Her

whole body was shaking. Boys could be so *vile*. Why was she even thinking about dating one? Ollie and Max were probably as bad as each other. No understanding or compassion between them. Just sneers and leers. *And* Ollie had apparently kissed Eve. Beautiful, stylish, tall Eve. Thinking of herself taking Eve's place was a joke.

Polly sensed a new atmosphere in the sober school corridors. People were gathered in groups, whispering together. There were smiles, and snatched glances, and low laughter. The whole school was buzzing with the news that Eve was a lesbian.

Eve will need our help to get through this, she thought. She pushed aside her worry over Ollie and started looking for her friends.

Polly bumped into Lila and Rhi by the lockers. She took them both by the arm and dragged them to a rarely used stairwell near the maths block where they could talk in peace.

"We need to talk," said Polly. "How—"

"How does everyone know about Eve?" Rhi finished Polly's question out of nowhere. "We were wondering the same thing."

"Rumours are like fungus," said Lila. "They grow out of nothing. I sent Eve a text this morning to warn her the news was out."

How would Eve feel about being the centre of gossip like this? Polly wondered anxiously. Eve was always so aware of what people thought of her.

"She's not coming to school today," Lila, went on, shaking her head. "This and that stuff in the paper have pretty much ruined her life. Dad was in such a temper this morning, I thought the roof was going to blow off. The wind outside didn't help."

Lila looked almost grey with tiredness. Polly closed her eyes. She'd almost forgotten about the newspaper article in this latest drama. "I wouldn't want to be Eve right now," she said with feeling. She knew just what it felt like to be the centre of nasty gossip.

"But how does everyone know?" Rhi repeated.

"Eve hasn't told anyone but the three of us," said Polly, looking at Rhi and Lila. Neither of them would have said anything, would they? "I didn't breathe a word. Did you?"

Rhi shook her head. "I may be mad at Eve right now, but I'd never gossip about her. No one deserves this."

"Eve confided in Ms Andrews," Lila said. "Do you think Ms Andrews told your mum, Polly?"

"You think my mum and Ms Andrews would have spread this?" Polly asked, feeling offended.

"I'm just eliminating possibilities, OK?"

"The newspapers have been snooping around the Somerstowns," said Rhi. "Your dad has too, Lila."

Lila looked angry. "This is all on my dad now, is it?"

Polly stepped in, trying to keep the peace. "Eve has been hanging out with Caitlin and her girlfriend Jessica recently. Maybe a journalist saw them together."

"Look," said Lila, "it doesn't matter how the rumour started. We all know it's true. It was bound to come out eventually."

"But it should have come from Eve," Polly pointed out unhappily.

That much was true. But there was nothing they could do about it now.

Polly felt her phone buzzing in her pocket. Her heart swooped at the thought that it might be Ollie, but then she immediately chastised herself as she saw the name on the screen. How could she be so self-centred when her friends were in trouble? "It's Eve," she said, looking up at the others.

"Put her on speakerphone," Lila suggested.

Polly tapped the button and held the phone so everyone could hear the conversation.

Eve sounded like she'd been crying. "Hi, Polly. Have you heard the news?"

"We all have, Eve," said Polly, as gently as she could. "Lila and Rhi are here. You're on speaker. How are you feeling? What do you want us to do?"

"Nothing," Eve sniffed. "It will all blow over, I guess. I'll just stay out of the way for a couple of days."

"Don't run away from this, Eve," Lila said, leaning into Polly's phone.

"Being gay is nothing to be ashamed of," Rhi added over Lila's shoulder.

"Come back," said Lila. "We'll look after you."

Polly looked at her friends, their two dark heads bent over her phone and the exact same look of concern on their faces. It looked as if they had both forgiven Eve for the many horrible things she'd done to them. Crises like these had a way of pulling friends together again.

"We could come over to yours after school if you like," Rhi suggested.

"Don't," said Eve at once. "Things are a bit . . . weird right now."

Polly guessed she was referring to the newspaper article. She shuddered to think of the atmosphere at the Somerstowns' house right now.

"But you're right, I can't run away from this," Eve said with a sigh. "I promise I'll see you all at school tomorrow."

"We can meet at mine and walk in together," Polly said. "If you want."

There was a moment of silence on the other end.

"Thanks," said Eve at last. "That's really kind of you, Polly. It would be nice to have some support. It's not going to be easy."

"We'll be here," said Lila.

"Thanks." Eve sounded unusually grateful. "I mean it. Thank you for being such good friends."

Polly clicked the off button on her phone and slid it slowly into her pocket. Life had changed so much since Lila had moved to Heartside Bay. The days when Eve and Lila had fought like cats, and

50

Rhi had screamed at Eve for taking Max, and Polly and Eve had fallen out – it all seemed a million years ago. They were friends now. Proper friends this time.

SEVEN

"Ready?" asked Polly.

Eve looked like she had been carved from a piece of stone. Her breathing was shallow and nervous. Polly had never seen her so scared.

"How do I look?" she said, licking her lips.

Eve's make-up was as perfect as ever, and her glossy auburn hair hung on her shoulders like red-gold satin. Compared to Eve, Polly felt like a scruffy little urchin, even though they were wearing the same school uniform. More acutely than ever, she felt the difference between herself and Eve.

"Gorgeous," said Lila. "I would fancy you if I was gay."

Eve gave a terrified smile. "I wish I could say the same of you, Lila."

"If you can make jokes," said Rhi, pressing Eve's arm in encouragement, "then you're as ready as you'll ever be."

"You do look amazing," Polly said honestly.

Eve pulled her lipgloss from her bag and swiped it across her lips. She straightened her shoulders and fussed with the lapels on her blazer. Then she nodded.

"Let's do this," she said.

They walked around the corner, towards the white steps that led to the reception area of Heartside High. Four of them in a row, arm in arm. Eve's head was held so high it was a wonder she could climb the steps without stumbling over her feet.

"Nice weather we're having," Lila commented.

"This isn't the time to talk about the weather," said Rhi through compressed lips.

"Just trying to make small talk."

Polly could see that Lila was almost as nervous as Eve.

"Only very boring people talk about the weather," said Eve through tight lips. "I am not a boring person. I give the best parties in Heartside Bay, whatever journalists might say."

"Hear, hear," said Rhi.

The steps seemed to go on for ever. People were starting to look, and whisper.

Eve detached herself from Polly and Rhi and pushed open the double doors.

"Good morning," she said, to the startled lady on reception.

"What are you doing, Eve? No one ever says hello to reception!" Lila hissed as Eve marched towards the corridor.

"I am not no one," said Eve with a glacial stare.

The corridor from the reception to their lockers had never felt so long. People were looking now – really looking. Stopping dead and pointing. Polly had to admire Eve's bravery as she strode on, hair bouncing glossily on her shoulders.

When they turned the corner, Polly felt Eve grip tightly at her hand. A group of year eight boys were hanging by the sports trophy cabinet, watching their approach. The boys sniggered.

"Lezzers," came the inevitable whisper as they walked past.

"Cockroaches," Eve responded smoothly, striding on.

How did she do it? Polly wondered in awe. How did Eve make the hardest thing in the world look completely effortless?

The only sign that Eve was struggling was the marble-white colour of her cheeks and the sensation of her long, beautifully manicured fingernails digging into Polly's skin. They were digging deep, and it hurt. Polly bit her lip and took the pain.

"Are you OK?" she whispered. "Do you want to leave?"

Eve shook her head wordlessly.

"Nearly there," said Lila.

"Keep going, Eve, you're doing brilliantly," Rhi said.

They reached the year ten lockers. The chattering crowd around the locker doors fell silent. Polly couldn't bring herself to look for Ollie, or Max, or any of their other friends among the watchful faces. Beside her, she felt Eve falter.

Eve's locker door had been covered in pictures of beautiful girls in swimsuits, draped over car bonnets and posing provocatively with glossy pouting lips. The word LESBIAN had been written in marker pen down the centre of her locker.

Lila and Rhi stood nervously by as Eve regarded her locker door. The world felt to Polly as if it was standing still.

Rhi reached for one of the pictures, her fingers curled and ready to tear it down.

"Don't," said Eve. A little colour had returned to her smooth cheeks. She seemed to be standing straighter, looking more like the Eve of old. "I quite like it."

There was a gasp, and a titter of laughter. Eve turned to face the crowd, flicking her hair back over her shoulders in the gesture Polly knew so well.

"I'm gay," she said with an elegant shrug. "It's hardly groundbreaking. Get over it."

There was a moment of shocked silence. Then someone laughed. It sounded warmer than the sniggering year eights. Eve's startling announcement seemed to have broken the tension.

The crowd slowly dispersed, heads together. Polly thought there was a more thoughtful air in the murmured conversations she could hear. She let out a breath she hadn't even realized she'd been holding.

"Whoa," said Lila, brushing her fringe out of her face. "That was intense."

Eve opened her locker door and started steadily placing her books in her bag. "It was," she said. "Wasn't it?"

"You were so cool, Eve," Rhi said, shaking her head with admiration.

"They don't call me the Ice Queen for nothing," Eve said, and gently closed her locker door.

A year eight girl Polly recognized was standing there, her hands pressed together, looking at Eve. Polly's heart jumped as she recognized her. The girl had got in Eve's way once, and earned one of Eve's famous put-downs. She wasn't the only person in the school Eve had been unpleasant to, Polly realized. Half the student body had suffered from Eve's jibes one way or another. Was this girl going to say something horrible? Enjoy a slice of perfect revenge?

Eve raised her eyebrows. "Did you want something?" she said, in the kind of voice that discouraged conversation.

The year eight girl looked Eve direct in the eye. "I wanted to thank you," she said.

Polly glanced at Rhi and Lila. She knew they were wondering the same thing. Had they heard right?

Eve was also looking confused. "You do?"

"You just did something really brave," said the year eight girl. "I saw the whole thing. I'm gay too, but I've never had the courage to tell anyone. And then I saw you stand there and face everyone and say that. It makes me feel like maybe I can say it too. Thank you."

Polly could see that Eve was struggling to find a response.

The girl was still looking at her. "You're a real inspiration, Eve," she said steadily.

Eve stepped towards the girl and hugged her.

"I'm glad," she said, holding her tightly. "Good luck. Don't worry about what people say. Your real friends will stand by you." She glanced at Polly, Lila and Rhi as she spoke. "Remember that."

"I will," said the girl gratefully.

Polly didn't think she'd ever felt so proud of anyone in her life.

EIGHT

Polly stood in front of the mirror curling her hair, gazing unseeingly at her reflection. It had been such a strange week. Half of it had felt unreal. Ollie and the locket, the newspaper and the whole thing with Eve at the lockers. Ollie had texted to apologize to her about being insensitive about Eve, and she had texted back to apologize for storming off. Rumours about people's sexuality were a sensitive subject for Polly, because of the hurtful things that had been said about her mum when she had come out as gay. She felt like Ollie should have realized that and been more understanding in the first place. But here she was on Friday evening, finally getting ready for the most important date of her life.

She felt as if she was going to be sick.

Something was wrong. Normal people didn't feel sick before going on dates. Polly reminded herself how long she'd wanted to go out with Ollie. It didn't seem to help. If anything, it made it worse. What if she'd built her whole life towards this moment, and then it all went wrong?

It's just normal nerves, she told herself. *Nothing more than that.*

But was it really normal to feel so shaky, and so sweaty, and so completely lost?

She put her hand to the locket around her neck. It felt warm against her palm. She hadn't taken it off since Ollie had given it to her.

She hadn't told anyone that Ollie had asked her out on a date yet. It still felt wrong to be happy when her friends were all in crisis.

She had put on more make-up than usual tonight, using a dark eyeshadow, lip liner and even false eyelashes. She wasn't entirely sure it suited her, but boys seemed to like girls who wore make-up. At least, if Eve was anything to go by.

She finished curling her hair. The black dye had

been a mistake, she knew that now. The starkness did nothing for the colour of her skin. But it was too late to change it for tonight.

Polly laid down her curling iron, put her head on her dressing table and groaned quietly. This was all too overwhelming. And she hadn't even started on her outfit.

I can't do this, she thought. *I have to cancel.*

But if she cancelled, Ollie might never ask her out again. He'd go out with one of the pretty football-team groupies that hung around at practice instead. Maybe it was better that way. They would be a better match, surely. Despite telling herself this, Polly's heart still leaped when there was a knock at the door. She dropped her phone with a clatter. Ollie was early!

She jumped up, and dashed frantically for her wardrobe. Grabbing a blue dress off its hook, she yanked it on and rushed down the stairs with her heart in her mouth. Could she tell him to his face that she didn't want to out with him any more? She quailed at the thought.

"Hi, Polly. Can I come in?"

Eve was through the front door before Polly'd had the chance to process that it wasn't Ollie at all. Polly pulled herself together with difficulty.

"Eve? Is everything OK?"

"No, everything's terrible." Eve was already halfway across the hall floor, one foot on the stairs. "Your room's up here, right? It's been a while since I was last here."

Polly followed Eve up the stairs.

"I remember this," said Eve, looking around at Polly's neatly ordered bedroom. "Not a sock out of place. Your room is the calmest place I've ever been."

Polly sat down at her desk as Eve seated herself at the end of the bed with her legs elegantly crossed.

"What happened to your face?" Eve asked, looking at Polly properly for the first time.

Polly decided not to answer that. "The more important question here is," she said, "what happened to *you*?"

"Where shall I start?" Eve sighed. "I came out to Daddy last week. He was completely brilliant about it, of course. But then my idiotic little sister heard the rumours at school today and told my mother when she got in from ballet, and she is a different story. She looked at me like I was some kind of alien."

Polly had a nasty feeling Eve was about to cry. "It's probably the shock," she said.

"When she stopped screaming at me, she said it was just a phase and I'd grow out of it," Eve said bitterly. "I told her sexuality wasn't an old pair of trousers."

Polly giggled in spite of herself. Only Eve could make comparisons between sexuality and fashion.

"Anyway, she's threatened to send me away until I come to my senses," said Eve, rolling her eyes. "It's all too embarrassing, apparently. How is she supposed to tell her friends?"

Polly felt a sudden deep stab of sympathy for Eve. She had always been quite close to her own mother. Although they fought sometimes, Polly knew she could talk to her mum about anything and her mum would always be there for her. It was clear that Eve and her mother had a very different kind of relationship.

Eve's chin wobbled. "I wanted to talk to Daddy about it, but he's so stressed and busy with work that I can't get five minutes alone with him. Mummy's already so freaked out about the bad publicity Daddy's getting in the papers that this has made her flip completely."

"That's awful," Polly murmured.

Eve pushed her hair back over her shoulders. "So basically, I wondered if I could stay with you," she said.

"You want to stay here?" said Polly in surprise.

"I can't go back home." There was a pleading look in Eve's steel-grey eyes. "Please let me stay."

"Of course," Polly said automatically. What else could she say? "Mum won't mind. We can put you in the spare room."

"I'd rather be in here with you," said Eve. Tears glistened in her eyes. "I don't want to be alone."

"Fine," said Polly. "I'll get the camp bed out."

Eve looked alarmed. "A camp bed? Is it horribly uncomfortable?"

Do you want to stay here or not? Polly thought, feeling a little irritated. "It's really comfortable," she assured Eve. "But we have an air bed too, if you'd prefer that."

"That sounds lovely," said Eve doubtfully. "Thank you, Polly. You're a real friend."

It took twenty minutes to locate the airbed, which had been stowed away in the loft. With some difficulty, Polly yanked it out from underneath a pile of coats and blankets, and tipped it down the loft ladder.

"Do you want a hand?" Eve asked as Polly attached the pump to the airbed valve and started pressing it down with her foot.

"Don't worry about it," said Polly. "I can do it. Did you have a bag?"

"I'll call my driver," said Eve, pulling out her phone. "He'll drop some bags round for me."

Pumping up the airbed was hard work. Polly had broken a sweat before it was half-full. Eve lay on Polly's bed, talking bitterly about the things her mother had said to her.

"She told me she was ashamed to be my mother. Charming. Chloe wasn't much better. She just giggled every time Mummy said the word 'lesbian'."

When the airbed was full at last, Polly fetched a sleeping bag from the airing cupboard and shook out the dust. Eve wrinkled her nose.

"It looks like the last person to use that sleeping bag

was Napoleon," she said, with a little laugh. "Luckily I don't have a dust allergy. We'll be as cosy as two bugs in a rug, won't we?"

Polly heard the doorbell for the second time that evening. Her stomach lurched. In all the drama with Eve, she'd forgotten about Ollie!

"Expecting someone?" said Eve, sitting gingerly on the airbed as if she expected it to burst on impact.

"Excuse me a minute," Polly said. Her heart was pounding so hard, she wouldn't have been surprised if it had jumped out of her mouth altogether.

Eve waved a hand. "Be my guest. I'll be here when you get back."

Polly hardly dared look at herself in the mirror. She had a nasty feeling her make-up had smudged in all the wrong places. The blue dress was now crumpled and marked with sweat patches from when she'd been pumping up the bed.

She slowly opened the front door.

Ollie looked a little startled. "What did you do to your face?"

"Make-up," Polly blurted. It was clear from the look on his face that it looked weird.

Ollie collected himself. "I hope you like roses," he said, holding them out.

He looked completely gorgeous, while she just looked like a clown. All of Polly's dreams felt like ashes in her mouth.

"I'm really sorry, Ollie," she gulped, holding on to the door. "I can't go out with you."

Ollie's face dropped. "What?"

"Tonight, I mean," Polly said quickly. "I can't go out with you tonight, Ollie, I'm really sorry. Eve is upstairs, and she's having a crisis. I have to be here for her."

Ollie lowered the flowers. "What do you want to help Eve for? She's never exactly been nice to you, Polly. This is our date. I've been looking forward to it. I thought you'd been looking forward to it too."

"She's my friend." Polly really wanted Ollie to understand. "And she needs me. She's staying here tonight."

"In your room?"

"Yes, in my room."

"You're not . . . becoming *attracted* to her, are you?" Ollie asked, with a funny look on his face.

Polly couldn't believe he'd just asked her that. How ignorant could you get? She felt a little strength seeping back into her.

"Being gay isn't contagious, you know," she said coolly.

"Right," said Ollie. He sounded unconvinced.

Polly felt on the verge of tears. Why was everything so hard? "Sorry about the date," she said quietly, closing the door on Ollie before she fell apart. She rested her head on the inside of the door and squeezed her eyes tightly shut. Didn't Ollie understand *anything*? How could he be the right guy for her if he really thought you could just become gay? As if it were a choice! She had no other option but to cancel the date. She had a friend who needed help. She wasn't the type of girl to just throw everything away for a boy. Maybe she and Ollie just weren't meant to be.

NINE

"Polly, I had no idea you had a date tonight." Eve looked concerned. "I'm really sorry if I messed things up."

"Don't worry about it," Polly said, suddenly realizing just how sad she felt about missing out on a date with the guy she'd liked for years.

"And with Ollie too! Who'd have thought you two would get together?"

There's nothing like rubbing salt into a wound, Polly thought sadly.

"You never dated Ollie, did you, Eve?" she asked. She had to be sure. You never really knew what was going on behind the scenes with Eve. The secretive way she had behaved with Max proved that.

"No." Eve gazed out of Polly's bedroom window and heaved a sigh. "I always thought Ollie and I *should* have dated. We would have looked great together."

Polly didn't really want to hear about how perfect Ollie and Eve looked together.

"But you did kiss him?" she pressed, as she folded up some clean laundry her mum had put at the end of her bed.

"Just a little peck," Eve said. "It didn't go anywhere. Tell me about you and Ollie, then. When did he ask you out?"

Polly wished she didn't feel so insecure about Eve and Ollie. She had too many other things to stress about in her life. "Wednesday," she said. "He gave me this."

"It's so pretty!" Eve exclaimed as Polly showed her the locket. "I didn't think Ollie had it in him to be so romantic. He must really like you."

But does he like me enough to ask me out again? Polly thought. Guys like Ollie had girls lining up for dates. Had she well and truly blown it?

"I really am grateful to you for letting me stay here," said Eve, reaching out to hug Polly. "It'll only be for a few days, I promise."

70

A few *days*? Polly hadn't realized Eve would be staying more than one night. She wondered uncomfortably what she'd started.

There was a loud hoot from the street.

"That'll be Paulo," said Eve, clapping her hands. "My driver. He'll have my bags."

Polly pulled back the curtain and stared out of the window. Eve's uniformed driver Paulo was unloading two *enormous* suitcases from the boot of the sleek, expensive car. He brought the suitcases up the stairs, puffing heavily as Eve issued instructions.

Within twenty minutes, Polly's bedroom was in chaos. The suitcases themselves took up half the room. Clothes lay in piles. Make-up was stacked high on Polly's desk. At least five pairs of shoes lay in a heap beside the airbed.

How many pairs of shoes does Eve need for "a few days"? Polly wondered.

"I'll have this part of your desk if that's OK," Eve said, waving at the bottles of shampoo and hair straighteners and bags of cotton wool that had joined the make-up.

Polly sat down on her bed. "Fine," she said helplessly.

Eve disappeared to the bathroom with a washbag the size of a briefcase.

"The mirror in your bathroom is really small, isn't it?" she said, returning a few minutes later. "How on earth do you manage?"

"It's amazing what you can do with just a little space," said Polly, staring forlornly at what was left of her desk.

Eve put her arm round Polly's shoulders. "Don't worry about Ollie," she said, giving Polly an encouraging shake. "Boys enjoy the thrill of the chase. It'll do him good if you turn him down a couple of times."

"I don't think he'll ask me out again," Polly said.

Eve rolled her eyes. "Of *course* he will. Believe me, Polly, I have a lot of experience in this kind of thing. Saying no when a boy asks you on a date makes them *more* interested in you, not less. It's a proven fact."

Polly could feel her anxiety welling up. "Can we not talk about this?" she said.

Eve wagged a manicured finger. "Just promise me you won't brood about it. Brooding means a poor night's sleep, and a poor night's sleep is *really* bad for your complexion. What's for dinner?"

They ordered pizza and decided to watch a movie. Polly's mum was out, so they made the most of the comfortable sitting room and the widescreen TV. The movie they watched wasn't that funny, but Eve's sarcastic commentary on it made Polly giggle helplessly. Eve could be great company when she wanted to be. It was nice, having a friend to chat with into the evening.

Maybe Eve staying here won't be so bad, Polly thought.

"Cup of tea?" she suggested when the movie had finished.

"Do you have something herbal?" said Eve, following Polly into the kitchen.

Polly peered into the cupboards. "We just have normal tea and normal coffee."

Eve made a face. "I'll make do with tea, I suppose."

Polly was reminded how Eve *could* be fun, but she could also be really annoying.

"You've been really kind to me tonight, Polly," said Eve as they headed upstairs to Polly's room with their tea. "I know I haven't been all that nice to you in the past, and I probably wouldn't have done the same for you if you were in my position. So thank you."

73

Polly felt gratified. "That's OK," she said. "It's what friends are for."

"That's my point." Eve looked uncomfortable. "I've never been a very good friend. I had no idea what it felt like until today, having people staring and whispering bad things about you. It's never happened to me before. I've seen it happen to others, though. I've *made* it happen to others." Eve paused. "I've really tortured people in the past, haven't I?"

There was no point in beating about the bush. "Yes," said Polly simply.

Eve made a face. "Tell it to me straight, why don't you?" she said with an awkward laugh. "Well, all that's about to change. I'm not going to bully anyone for being different, ever again. I don't want anyone to feel how I felt today."

"Was it really bad?" Polly asked. "You seemed really cool about it."

"I hope I never go through anything like that, ever again."

Polly was moved by the pain in Eve's eyes. The Ice Queen was melting.

"It probably isn't over yet," she said, pressing Eve's

hand. "It'll take a while for people to stop talking. But you've made a really good start. It's going to improve from now on."

"Thank you," said Eve quietly. "I'll hold on to that thought."

They got ready for bed. Eve took almost half an hour in the bathroom, but Polly found that she didn't mind tonight. Eve had really opened up to her, and Polly realized what a rare thing that was. Polly felt confident that Eve meant every word she'd said. She was going to change, and become a better person.

If someone like Eve could change, maybe Polly could too. Be more confident, less prone to worrying about things.

Maybe she and Ollie needn't be such a hopeless match after all.

TEN

Saturday was bright and warm.

A perfect day for a wedding, Polly thought.

Leaving Eve watching TV, she got her things together and headed out into the sunshine. She and Lila were working for Mr Gupta today, waitressing at a big wedding reception in the grounds of Heartwell Manor. Rhi would be there too, as a wedding singer. She had a great voice, and got plenty of singing work at weekends for all the weddings that Heartside Bay was famous for. Polly wondered briefly if Eve had ever had a job. *No way*, she thought. Why would she, when her father was so rich?

"Ready to dress up?" Polly asked when Lila opened the front door at her first knock.

Liila pushed her glossy brown hair out of her eyes and looked eagerly at the bag over Polly's arm. "Are those our outfits?"

The theme for today's wedding was *The Great Gatsby*. Polly adored the twenties style: flapper dresses, feathered headbands, long jangly beads. She had worked hard on three perfect dresses for her, Lila and Rhi to wear.

"Polly, it's *gorgeous*," Lila gasped as Polly carefully took her dress out of its bag. "How do you do it?"

Polly felt pleased. "It wasn't difficult," she said as Lila took off her clothes and wriggled into the pale green shift dress with its feathered fringe, twirling ecstatically in front of her bedroom mirror. "I bought the feathered fringing at the haberdasher and just stitched it on. There's a headband to match, look. And—"

She opened her coat so Lila could see the matching silver feathery dress she was wearing.

"I've made Rhi a red dress with black bead fringing sewn around the neckline," Polly went on, "with an adorable little close-fitting hat. Red looks so great on her."

"She'll *love* it," said Lila, gazing at the red dress with awe.

They agreed to fix their hair and make-up at Heartwell Manor. Mr Gupta wanted them to be there for three o'clock, and time was running out.

The marquee looked decadent. The walls were swathed in pale green silk, with silver chandeliers hanging from the ceiling. Tables were laid with silvery tablecloths, and a pyramid of champagne flutes stood in the centre of the room.

Rhi was there already, looking nervous and talking to Brody the guitar player and the rest of the band. Her wild, cloudy curls had been tamed so that they lay slicked to her head in a twenties style. Brody Baxter scrubbed up well, Polly realized, in a black tuxedo and a bow tie. His long blond hair was as wild and surfy as ever though.

"I'm so terrified," Rhi whimpered when she saw Polly and Lila.

"You are going to be incredible," Lila assured her.

"And you'll *look* incredible too," Brody said with a whistle as Polly handed Rhi her black and red dress.

Rhi vanished behind a curtain to change.

"Quickly now," Mr Gupta urged Polly and Lila, rushing past in his white tuxedo. "Canapés on the silver trays. Champagne will be poured when the brides arrive."

"Brides, as in plural?" said Polly, turning to Lila in surprise.

"Sounds that way." Lila had already put her headband on and was halfway through her make-up. "Hurry up, Polly, the guests will be here in a minute."

Polly barely had time to put on her own headband and lay the canapés in neat rows on the trays when the sound of popping champagne bottles filtered through the curtains separating the wedding party from the catering area. The brides and their guests had arrived.

As Polly moved through the happy chattering crowd with her silver tray, the band began to play.

Polly looked up to the stage and watched as Rhi, glittering in her red and black dress, began to sing, her eyes closed as she swayed back and forth.

Brody was at the piano; the other members of the band on drums and sax. Rhi leaned on the piano as she sang classic twenties songs, smiling into Brody's eyes as if no one else was in the room. Their connection was almost visible, a shining thread holding them together.

Rhi and Brody would make such a great couple, Polly thought, gazing dreamily at the stage. What would it take to convince Rhi that Brody was a far better fit for her than Max?

The brides looked incredible as they moved among their guests, talking and laughing in matching gauzy golden gowns. The food was disappearing fast.

"More food," Mr Gupta urged. "Quickly, Polly!"

Polly realized there was only one canapé left on her tray. She hurried back to the catering area to collect some more.

"How did I sound?" said Rhi, snapping off her mic as he put her head through the catering curtain during a break in the music.

"As great as I said you would," said Lila. "You should totally date Brody."

Rhi flushed. "I'm going out with Max!"

Polly rushed in. "Lila's right, Rhi. Brody is perfect for you. Just looking at you both on the stage . . .

there's a kind of magic about it. You should give him a chance!"

Rhi squirmed. "Brody and I have started writing songs together," she said shyly. "I want to have a collection of original tracks to send to a record producer really soon. But any connection that we have is only through our music. He'd never like someone like me. Besides," she added as Lila and Polly started protesting, "I wouldn't want to risk our working relationship by . . . turning it into something else."

Polly opened her mouth to argue. Mr Gupta put his head around the curtain.

"What is this dawdling?" he demanded. "Where are my canapés?"

Polly grabbed her tray and hurried back out among the guests.

Polly stifled a yawn as she cleared away the plates from the tables. The reception would continue into the morning hours, but her and Lila's food service duties were done. Polly was looking forward to going home and putting her feet up. Maybe Eve had talked to her mother by now, and would be back home. Polly hoped so.

She had been discreetly checking her phone throughout the wedding reception for any missed calls from Ollie. Nothing. Whatever Eve said, Polly was convinced that he wouldn't call again. *It's for the best,* she reminded herself. *We would never have worked out.*

Lila was clearing tables a short distance away.

Polly wished she could talk to Lila about Ollie. But how could she? It would be far too weird to ask advice from Ollie's former girlfriend.

"Psst!"

Polly glanced round in surprise. Eve was smiling at her through the tent flaps.

"Hey," Eve whispered. "We thought we'd sneak in. I could use some fun."

Polly glanced around. No one was watching. "It's a private wedding party, Eve," she said a little reluctantly. "Who are you with?"

Eve grinned. She tugged back the marquee flap a little further – to reveal Ollie and Josh.

Colour whooshed into Polly's cheeks. Ollie was

looking right at her. Eve had brought him here. For her. She put down the dirty plates she was holding in case she dropped them.

Eve slipped through the tent flaps, tugging Ollie and Josh with her. She smoothed down the pretty pale blue dress she was wearing. "I hope this is Gatsby enough," she said, giggling. "I have the most divine dress at home but of course I couldn't sneak back and fetch it."

"I hope they had hoodies in the twenties," said Josh, tweaking his sweatshirt. "Nice party," he added, looking at the dance floor in admiration.

"Rhi sounds fantastic," said Ollie, looking at where Rhi was still singing on the stage with Brody.

"I don't know what the brides will say to gatecrashers," said Lila, appearing behind Polly.

Eve looked shocked. "Brides?" she said. "This . . . this is a gay wedding?"

She looked at the two golden brides dancing with each other in the middle of the floor, their heads on each other's shoulders. They looked so in love.

"Well, this is awkward," said Ollie, loudly.

Eve paled. Polly had spent the whole wedding

wanting Ollie to get in touch. Now all she wanted to do was kick him for being an insensitive idiot. Eve was clearly uncomfortable enough, did Ollie really have to point it out to everyone? Once again, the question raised its head. How could she ever go out with someone like Ollie?

"Do you want to go home, Eve?" she said stiffly. "Our shift is almost over."

Eve was watching the brides as they danced. "Are their parents here?" she asked.

Lila pointed to a table of older people, all sitting together and talking over bottles of wine. Eve sat down at the nearest table. She looked almost winded.

"Maybe there's hope for me yet," she said.

Brody broke into a rousing tune that saw a surge of people heading for the dance floor.

"Catchy," said Josh. Polly saw his eyes flicker towards Lila.

Polly chanced a glance at Ollie, and saw that he was looking at her steadily. "Dance?" he said.

Polly took his hand and followed him to the dance floor in a daze. This was unexpected. Was he giving her another chance? What would happen now?

Rhi had joined in on the song. She sang with Brody, their feet tapping the stage in rhythm.

It was impossible to resist the Charleston beat. Josh had joined them now, and Lila too. Polly threw herself into the music, whirling under Ollie's arms and stamping her feet with the rest of the room.

"Wow," said Eve breathlessly as the song came to an end and the room broke into cheers. "I am *so* having a twenties theme for my next party. Who's coming?"

"Me!" Ollie said, laughing.

"Fine, twist my arm," said Josh.

The tempo changed. Brody and Rhi segued into a slow song that had couples moving closer together on the dance floor.

"Nothing like a song about broken hearts to get the party going," said Josh.

Ollie was about to pull Polly towards him. But she didn't know what to say to him – should she apologize for turning him away last night? Or wait for him to say something? Polly's hands were sweaty. Desperate for a distraction, she grabbed Josh's hand instead.

"Ask Lila to dance," she said in a low voice.

"I don't know where she is," said Josh, blushing.

"She's right here. . ." Polly's voice trailed away. Lila had been dancing beside her just a moment ago, but now she'd gone.

"There!" Polly pointed towards a pale green feathery headdress across the dance floor. She gave Josh a little push in the small of the back, propelling him across the marquee to where Lila was standing by the bar. "Go on! What have you got to lose?"

"Fine," Josh sighed. "I'll ask her. Wish me luck."

You won't need luck.

The words died before they reached Polly's lips as the people on the dance floor shifted and they could see Lila more clearly. Leaning across the bar, oblivious to the fact she was being watched, Lila was kissing the bartender.

"Right," said Josh, turning back around. In an agony of embarrassment, Polly caught him by the arm.

"Don't think badly of Lila, Josh. She's still grieving about Ryan. She's confused. . ."

Josh shook her hand off. "Maybe Lila isn't the girl I thought she was."

Lila pulled back from the bartender, laughing. She

stopped abruptly as she saw Josh's back disappearing through the crowd. As Polly caught her eye, she looked furious.

Polly had a horrible feeling she had just put her nose where it wasn't wanted.

ELEVEN

There was a burst of applause. People in the room were standing up around their tables, clapping hard as Rhi and Brody took their final bows, smiling and waving, and prepared to leave the stage.

When Polly looked back at the bar, Lila and the bartender had disappeared.

"Lila?"

Polly pushed through the guests, hunting for Lila's distinctive feathered headpiece.

I practically ordered Josh to find Lila, she thought in an agony of shame. *Now Josh is embarrassed and Lila's mad with me.* She'd pushed Josh and Lila further apart than ever.

When would she learn to stop meddling in other people's lives?

The disco had started up again, a thumping tune that cleared the tables and got everyone on the dance floor. Polly spotted Eve dancing by the stage, surrounded by girls.

"Polly!" Eve waved. "Come and meet my new friends Pip, Louise and Nan."

Pip and Louise were both blonde and small and looked like they were an item. Very tall and striking and apparently on her own, raven-haired Nan was wearing a slim red column dress that made her skin look like beautiful marble.

"We love your dress," said Pip, stroking the feathers on Polly's hemline enviously.

"Gorgeous," Louise agreed.

"Dance with us," Eve coaxed, holding out her hands to Polly.

Nan was looking at Polly in a distinctly unwelcoming way.

Oh my gosh, Polly realized. *Nan thinks I'm with Eve!* If she hadn't been so worried about Lila, it would have been funny.

"Thanks, but I have to go and find Ollie," she said.

"Don't chase him, Polly," Eve said, twirling around

89

her. Nan seemed to relax at the word "him". "If he's keen, he'll come to you. Take it from me, I'm an expert."

Another tune burst from the decks. With a shout of happy recognition, the energy in the marquee went up several degrees. As Eve whirled away into the heart of the dance floor, Polly felt a hand slip into hers.

"Hey, gorgeous," said Ollie, pulling her close. "I thought I'd lost you." He looked questioningly at her and she willed him silently not to bring up last night.

"Dance?" he asked, for the second time.

Polly sighed in relief and smiled her assent. She wasn't quite ready to talk about her conflicted feelings with Ollie yet, but she could at least dance with him. Maybe it wasn't such a bad thing that Ollie didn't overthink everything the way she did.

Ollie was an enthusiastic dancer. Polly found it hard not to giggle as he bounced around the floor, punching the air and singing along to the words.

"Channelling Tigger?" she teased.

"Cheeky," said Ollie. "Come here."

He reached out his arms. Polly had dreamed about a moment just like this.

A movement over Ollie's shoulder distracted her. A face was peeking through by the tent flaps.

Max.

Polly hunted for Rhi in the crowd. There she was, over by the edge of the stage, standing close to Brody. *Very* close to Brody. Brody had his arm loosely around Rhi's waist, and was whispering something in her ear that was making her laugh. If they could be left alone for just a short while longer, Polly felt confident Rhi and Brody could get it together. At last, Rhi would have a boyfriend that she deserved.

Max can't see Rhi with Brody, Polly thought. *It'll ruin everything.*

Polly looked at Ollie, standing there with his arms reaching towards her. She sighed.

"Just give me a second," she said. "OK?"

Polly's eyes were trained on Max as she bore down on him.

"Hi, Max!" she said brightly, making sure that she was standing directly between Max and any view he might have of Rhi and Brody together by the stage. "What are you doing here?"

"Looking for Rhi," said Max, peering over Polly's

shoulder. "She said she'd be finished with this by eleven. Have you seen her?"

Polly seized Max by the arm and marched him out of the tent. "Sorry, she already left."

Max frowned. "But she said—"

"You know how these things go," Polly prattled on a little nervously. She prayed that Rhi and Brody weren't about to appear through the tent flaps hand in hand. "She sang a great set, but she was pretty tired when it was over. She, uh, said to tell you she'd see you tomorrow."

Max's eyes were fixed on two girls kissing in the shadows outside the marquee. "Is this, like, a lesbian wedding or something?"

"Yes," said Polly. When would Max get the hint? "See you tomorrow, OK?"

Max obediently turned round and headed for the street. There was still a puzzled look on his face. Polly breathed a sigh of relief.

"Now what?"

Polly spun round, her hand on her heart. "Ollie! You gave me the fright of my life! What are you doing, sneaking up on me like that?"

"I followed you," Ollie said. He was looking hurt. "I wanted to know what was so important that it took you away." He gazed after Max's disappearing back. "So what were you doing out here talking to Max when you're supposed to be dancing with me?"

"It was Rhi and Brody," Polly explained. "I had to get Max out of the way before he saw them together."

"Rhi and Brody?" Ollie repeated. "Rhi's going out with Max, Polly. What's Brody got to do with this?"

"Max isn't right for Rhi," Polly said in a rush. "He's a cheat and a liar. I want her to be happy. She and Brody are perfect for each other."

Ollie was beginning to frown now. "Max is my friend, Polly," he said. "I know he's a handful, but what gives you the right to meddle in his life?"

Polly was determined that Ollie should understand. "I want Rhi to be happy. She's had too much sadness in her life, Ollie. Doesn't she deserve someone better than Max?"

His eyes sparked. He looked angry. "First you have to be there for Eve. Then you have to set up Lila and Josh. And now you're sabotaging Max and Rhi's relationship?"

It didn't sound too good when Ollie put it like that, Polly realized. Maybe he wasn't the only insensitive one.

"They're my friends," she said feebly. "I'm just trying to take care of them."

Ollie's expression softened. "Someone should take care of you for a change."

His face was very close out here in the moonlight. Polly felt a little breathless.

"Are you volunteering for the job?" she asked.

Ollie pulled her closer. "If you'll have me," he said.

"Yes."

A strain of music floated out of the marquee, into the dark gardens of Heartwell Manor.

"Can we have that dance now?" Ollie said.

Polly laid her head on Ollie's chest, snuggling into him. He folded his arms around her back. The music was dreamy, almost otherworldly, spilling into the warm night around them. As if it were being played for them alone.

"I always loved this song," Ollie murmured, his lips close to Polly's ear.

"Me too," Polly whispered back.

Ollie's lips were trailing from her ear across her cheek now. Little warm kisses, one after the other. Polly's skin tingled all over.

Nothing else matters, she thought. *Ollie's going to kiss me. . .*

There was a clattering sound, the crunch of shoes on gravel. Polly jerked back, her mouth inches from Ollie's.

"There you are, Polly!" said Eve, putting her hands on her hips. "I've been looking *everywhere* for you."

TWELVE

"Come on," said Eve briskly. "You're needed."

Polly's face was aflame. She wanted the ground to swallow her up. Couldn't Eve see that she'd interrupted a really important moment? Didn't Eve feel any embarrassment at all?

"Hey," Ollie said indignantly. "We're busy here, Eve. Do you mind?"

"Sorry, Ollie, but this can't wait." Eve seemed completely unembarrassed. "It's really important that Polly comes right now. You two can talk later."

"I'd better go," Polly muttered to Ollie.

Ollie looked resigned. He kissed her cheek and let go of her hand. "Go on then. But you owe me a date *and* a moonlit dance now. And I plan to collect very soon."

"Come *on*," said Eve.

She dragged Polly back into the marquee, through the dancing guests, past the half-eaten cake and around the side of the stage until they reached the catering area where Eve finally dropped Polly's arm.

"Eve, what are you doing?" Polly hissed furiously, rubbing at her wrist. "What is so important that you had to do that?"

"I was saving you from yourself." Eve spun Polly round and wagged a finger in her face. "What did I tell you about chasing Ollie?"

Polly was struggling to hold it together. This was feeling distinctly surreal. "What? I wasn't chasing him, Eve. He came after *me*. He—"

"Was about to kiss you, I know." Eve looked exasperated. "Haven't you heard a word I've said to you about boys? You have to take things *slowly*."

Polly took a very deep breath. "Is anyone bleeding? Or dying? Or crying?"

"Not yet," said Eve significantly.

That was it? Eve had dragged Polly away from the most romantic moment of her life to save her from Ollie?

You needed saving, said the little voice in Polly's head. *You're not right together.*

But for once, Polly was too frustrated to listen.

"Eve, that was completely out of order! What Ollie and I were about to do is none of your business!"

"But it *is* my business," Eve corrected. "You're my friend. Friends watch out for each other. And you were about to make the biggest mistake of your life. You have to play it cooler than this, Polly. It's coming across as needy and, frankly, unattractive."

Polly felt as if she had been punched in the stomach. Was she coming across as needy? Eve had dated far more boys than Polly, so maybe she did know what she was talking about. Polly felt sick at the thought that Ollie might think she was desperate or unattractive.

"I'm telling you this for your own good," said Eve, linking arms with Polly. "Ollie's going to be even keener now. I promise you. Let's go home. You look exhausted. I'm sure waitressing can't be good for you."

Polly did feel pretty exhausted, now she came to think about it. *It's good for my bank balance, though*, she thought numbly. *Not a problem Eve will ever have to worry about.*

"Great work," said Mr Gupta happily, handing Polly a crinkling brown envelope full of banknotes. "This has been a very good event. Not a hitch. The brides look so happy, don't they?"

Polly glanced at the brides, dancing cheek to cheek on the dance floor in a world of their own.

"This is why I am in the wedding business," said Mr Gupta. There was a misty look in his eye. "To witness such moments is a privilege. Life would be too hard without love."

Polly fetched her coat and said goodbye to the others, thinking about what Mr Gupta had said. She couldn't imagine life without love. Love was the only thing that made it all worthwhile. Would she lose Ollie by doing what Eve told her? She liked Ollie, she always had. And she knew that he liked her too. But it felt like every time they met up something went wrong. It should have been simple but she couldn't stop the thoughts in her head. She second-guessed him and herself until she didn't know what to do.

Eve was waiting for her outside the doors of the hotel. So was Paulo, Eve's driver, the door to the car open and waiting.

I guess there are perks to having a friend like Eve, Polly thought, glad to settle into the plush interior of the car. *Even when she insists on ruining my life.*

"Some of those girls were getting really flirty with me at the party, don't you think?" Eve looked pleased with herself as Paulo pulled away from the hotel. She lowered her voice. "Nan in particular. Of course I'm not ready for any of that just yet, but it's good to know that I haven't lost my touch just because the scenery has changed."

Eve chattered on about the wedding as they drove. The dresses, the music, the brides. Polly let it flow over her like water.

At the front door, Polly's phone buzzed. She took her phone out of her pocket.

Next Friday? No interruptions this time xx

Polly stared at the message. Maybe Eve was right. Pushing Ollie away seemed to be making him keener.

Her fingers automatically started typing a reply.

Yes! I promise that—

Eve plucked the phone from Polly's hands before she could finish typing and slipped it into her own handbag.

"Don't answer him yet," she said. "Let him stew."

Polly opened the front door slowly, letting Eve into the house first. These games felt all wrong. They weren't her at all.

Halfway up the stairs, Eve swung round and clapped her hands. "You know something? All the music and dancing tonight has given me the most *fabulous* idea. Why don't we all go away for the weekend?"

"All of us?" said Polly. "The boys too?"

Eve pulled a face. "No *way*, they would only make trouble. Girls only. With all the awful business with Ryan and the papers, we could really use a break from dreary old Heartside. What about camping at the Funky Fox? It's on next weekend. I'm sure I can get us tickets."

Polly felt excited. She'd always wanted to check out the Funky Fox. Great bands always headlined the festival, which came to the hills just outside Heartside every year, and she'd heard the vintage clothes stalls were second to *none*.

"The Funky Fox sold out months ago!" Polly protested.

Eve waved the problem aside like an irritating fly. "You can always get tickets if you have the money. Leave it to me. We'll camp out, and have a fire, and eat marshmallows, and dance until we drop. We can go there straight after school on Friday and stay until Sunday night. What do you think?"

Polly wavered. Going to the Funky Fox with the girls on Friday meant that she would have to turn down Ollie's date. Her stomach lurched with disappointment.

"Don't give me that moon face, Polly," Eve said. "You need time to chill out and forget about boys. Just us and the music. Don't you think it would be great?"

Polly pictured the music, and the atmosphere, and the great views up on Hilltop Farm where the Funky Fox took place. She hadn't been camping in years. It would be fun, she knew. And her friends needed a break. She should be there for them.

Ollie would have to wait.

THIRTEEN

The next morning Polly lay on her bed, listening to the water run as Eve took her shower. She'd been in there for a good forty minutes now, and Polly was desperate to wash her hair.

She whiled away the wait by thinking of Ollie. His wide shoulders, his heartbreaking smile. The locket she still wore around her neck. She hadn't taken it off since Ollie had given it to her. It was like a talisman. Proof that everything would work out fine. Somehow.

She just had to break the news to Ollie about Friday. Swinging her legs off the bed, Polly padded over to Eve's bag and started hunting for her phone. Tissues, lipsticks, a pink leather diary, a purse containing about four credit cards. Polly couldn't help but whistle as she stared at the gold one. What must it be like, she wondered, not having to worry about money for a single minute?

No phone. Eve had hidden it well. Polly sat down on the bed again. If Eve took much longer, she would have to take a wash downstairs in the kitchen sink.

"That's better," said Eve, padding back into the bedroom in a pure white towelling robe. Her auburn hair hung in shiny wet tendrils down her back. "Steaming your pores is so important. I try and do it every day."

Finally, Polly thought. She sat up.

"Can I go in the bathroom now?"

"What a silly question! It's your house, Polly," Eve said generously. "Of course you can. Oh, wait, I need to floss."

Ten more minutes passed. Polly tried not to feel too irritated when Eve swanned out of the bathroom again, running her tongue over her perfect white teeth.

"So what are we going to do today?" Eve asked brightly. She surveyed her clothes, which lay in tangled heaps all over Polly's carpet. It had taken every bit of Polly's self-control not to pick them up and fold them and arrange them in neat piles. "It would be good to know *before* I get dressed so I can be sure of wearing the right thing."

"We don't normally do much on Sundays," said Polly, tearing her eyes from Eve's mountain of clothes and eyeing the bathroom longingly.

"I'll think of something fun," said Eve. "How about—"

"Going in the bathroom now," said Polly.

She shut the bathroom door, and looked around in dismay. *More* mess. The tiny room looked like a bomb had hit it. Dripping shampoo bottles lay on their sides in the tub. The shower curtain was soaked and hanging out of the bath, water dripping and puddling on the bath mat.

Polly found the only dry part of the bathroom floor and stood there, breathing hard.

Stay calm, she instructed herself.

The fact remained that Eve had needed a place to stay and Polly had offered. It was what friends did. Friends shouldn't get worked up over damp towels, she knew, but she couldn't help herself. How much longer would Eve be staying? She needed space to *think*.

Polly located the only dry towel and laid it out on the chair. Then she climbed into the shower and turned on the taps. She closed her eyes, waiting for the familiar soothing, warm whoosh to come out of the shower attachment.

"Aaargh!"

The water was stone cold.

"Is Eve still getting up?" Polly's mum peered up the stairs at the sound of banging and crashing.

Polly helped herself to a third piece of toast. She needed it, after the coldest shower she'd ever experienced. "It's not easy, looking like Eve," she said.

Her mother put her hands on her hips. "Do you know how long she's going to stay, Polly? I don't mean to be a bad host, but I'm not sure this house can cope with Eve for much longer."

"I'm not sure *I* can cope with Eve for much longer," Polly sighed.

Her mother regarded her. "Getting a bit much, is she?"

"I like Eve," Polly said helplessly. "Really, I do.

She's hard work but she's basically a kind person. She doesn't mean to be annoying. She just . . . is."

"Why don't I call Beth and take you girls to the shops?"

Polly looked gratefully at her mother. "Would you do that?"

"Of course I would," said her mother. "I could use a new work jacket. And Beth wants to show me some cushions she's thinking of getting. Let's all go down to the high street this morning and have some fun."

"Did someone say shopping?" said Eve, gliding into the kitchen. Her hair lay in perfect curls on her shoulders, and her white shirt looked as crisp as a layer of freshly fallen snow.

Polly tried to smile. "Mum and Beth are offering to take us into town today. What do you think?"

"That's *so* kind, I'd *love* that." Eve clapped her hands. "I know! I'll buy everyone something special. As a way of saying thank you for having me to stay."

Polly's mother looked startled. "Really, Eve, there's no need to—"

"I insist," said Eve. She sat down at the kitchen table and looked at the teapot with its chipped spout.

"How about a new teapot? I'm sure I could find you a lovely one."

"I quite like the one we've got, thanks," said Polly's mum. "It's full of memories."

And tea, Polly thought.

"You really don't need to buy anything for us, Eve," her mum continued. "It's been a pleasure having you."

"Well, I will anyway," said Eve, looking determined. "And I'll buy you something too, Polly. There is a darling new boutique that's opened on Marine Parade with the most glorious cashmere. We can go there."

Polly caught her mother's eye. Cashmere wasn't really her thing.

"That's very kind of you, Eve," said Polly's mum with a sigh. "We'd love to accept. I'll just call Beth and tell her to meet us at the Ciao Café in what, half an hour?"

FOURTEEN

Polly sat a little further down in her chair. She wished Eve hadn't chosen the window seat in the café. Everyone walking down Church Road and along the high street could see them all sitting there. Eve and Polly's mum and Ms Andrews and her. She'd seen at least five people she recognized from school poke each other and whisper at the sight of Polly's mum and their history teacher with Eve.

"Is everything all right, Polly?" said Polly's mum, noticing.

"I just dropped my napkin," Polly mumbled.

She knew it was wrong to feel this embarrassed. So her mum was dating her history teacher. And the whole school was gossiping about Eve's sexuality. So what?

Why did any of it matter?

As Polly straightened up, she was surprised to see tears rolling down Eve's cheeks. She'd obviously missed something important in the conversation.

"People can be so unkind," said Polly's mother with feeling.

Ms Andrews nodded in agreement. "If the world were more open to difference, it would be a much happier place. How have you been coping?"

Two year eleven boys gawped through the window at their table, threw their heads back and roared with laughter. Polly died yet another death.

"It hasn't been great," Eve admitted, dabbing at her cheeks with a balled-up napkin. "Coming right after the awful tragedy with Ryan, and Daddy being in the papers, and all those horrible things the journalist said about how irresponsible I was. And then the gay thing at school, and my mum's awful reaction. It's been tough."

Polly's mother and Ms Andrews murmured sympathetically. Polly sat, frozen with guilt, scolding herself for being so hard on Eve. Had she forgotten all the problems Eve had been dealing with lately? She resolved to be more patient with her. After coffee, they split up. Eve and Polly headed to some of the clothes shops along the front, while Polly's mum and Ms Andrews went to the homeware store on Church Road to look at cushions.

"This is the place I was talking about this morning," said Eve, seizing Polly's hand and dragging her towards a little shop. "Come on, let's see if I can find you something nice."

Polly sat on the small spindly chair at the back of the shop as Eve exclaimed over the shining chrome rails of little beaded tops and trousers. This wasn't the kind of place Polly was used to shopping in. Everything looked too perfect. Even a little boring, if she was honest. Polly enjoyed bright colours and fun patterns.

A price tag brushed against her face. She glanced absently at the tag.

A hundred and fifty pounds for a cardigan? Polly thought, glued to her chair. That was insane.

"Here," Eve said, thrusting a thin sea-green jumper into Polly's arms. "Just your colour. Have you thought about dying your hair again? I'm not sure the black works with your skin tone. A softer blonde would be better. That's your natural colour, isn't it?"

Polly's palms felt damp. She hardly dared touch the cardigan, imagining sweaty handprints all over the delicate fabric. "It's not really . . . me, Eve," she managed to say, gingerly hanging it back up again.

"Shame," Eve sighed.

A phone buzzed in Eve's pocket.

Eve reached into her pocket and took out Polly's phone. She looked at the screen and tutted. "Ollie again."

Polly reached for her phone. "Please, Eve, let me at least see it!" she said.

"Play it cool," Eve instructed, pocketing the phone. "Remember?"

Polly gritted her teeth. "If you're going to keep my phone hostage, Eve, then at least let me take you to my kind of shop," she said.

Eve grumbled but let Polly drag her back out on to Marine Parade again.

"Where were you thinking of?" she said.

"There's a great charity shop on Church Road," said Polly.

Eve's face fell. "Second-hand clothes? You have to be kidding."

Polly felt a little more in control now they'd left the cashmere shop. "My favourite vintage store's right next door. We'll do them both. Trust me, Eve. I know what I'm doing."

How often has Eve said that to me in the past few days? Polly wondered. It felt good to be dishing out the same medicine.

Eve stood uncertainly in the middle of the Happy Hospice shop as Polly rifled through the rails.

"It smells in here," she complained. "Do you often shop in this place?"

"All the time. What do you think of this jumper?"

Polly held up a thickly knitted blue and white striped jumper. It would look fun over the pink button-down shirt she'd found the last time she'd come to the Happy Hospice. She could see that Eve was struggling for something nice to say.

"Come on then," she said, relenting. She put the jumper back. "We'll try Truly Vintage next door."

Truly Vintage had started as a market stall behind the high street. With the recent surge of interest in vintage clothing, it had moved to its current premises on Church Road. It was Polly's favourite shop in the whole of Heartside Bay.

"You have to admit, this is adorable," Polly coaxed, lifting a little green sequinned blouse off the rail by the window and holding it up for Eve to admire.

"It's quite Gatsby, I suppose," Eve said, tilting her head to one side.

Polly could hear buzzing sounds coming from Eve's pocket. One, two, three buzzes. Three texts on her phone. Were they all from Ollie?

"I don't think anyone's ever worn it. Try it on," Polly said, pressing the Gatsby blouse into Eve's arms. "Go on, the changing room's lovely, really light and spacious. And you could try this too. And this."

Polly pressed a grey jacket with military-inspired buttons and a black and gold art deco patterned skirt into Eve's hands. They were both a bit more quirky than Eve would have gone for on her own, but Polly could tell Eve was intrigued.

"Fine," Eve sighed. She shrugged off her coat and handed it to Polly. "Hold on to this, will you?"

As soon as Eve swished the curtain shut, Polly took

her phone out of Eve's coat pocket and checked her messages.

Still waiting for an answer

Can't wait until Friday

Meet me after football Mon?

STILL WAITING! xx

Polly wanted to sing with happiness. Didn't she deserve a little happiness? If she could just stop overthinking everything, maybe she and Ollie *could* work out. She stroked the kisses at the bottom of his fourth text, grinning foolishly to herself. If she was quick, she could answer before Eve came out of the changing room.

Mon after football sounds good.
Can't wait.

She hesitated. Was "can't wait" a bit needy? Should

she add kisses?

"Are you ready?" Eve called from the changing room.

There was no more time. Polly swiftly tapped send and put the phone back as Eve pulled back the curtain.

The sequinned blouse looked gorgeous with Eve's hair, and the jacket fitted her slender shoulders perfectly. "I love these," Eve confessed, stroking the jacket and blouse. "But the skirt isn't very me."

Polly wondered if Eve could see the guilt on her face. *It's my life*, she reasoned. *Not Eve's. If I want to go out with Ollie, I can.*

"Try the blouse and jacket with this instead," she suggested, passing Eve a dark blue high-waisted skirt.

"Polly, you are clever," Eve marvelled, checking her new reflection out in the mirror five minutes later. The skirt made her long legs look endless. "How did you know this would look so good? And it's so cheap!"

Polly blushed, feeling pleased. "I'm glad you like it. Now can we go back to the Happy Hospice? I'm still thinking about that striped jumper."

It was past lunchtime when they emerged from the Happy Hospice. Polly had found a round-collared blouse that she decided would look even better with the striped jumper than the button-down.

"This has been the best shopping day ever," Eve announced as they started walking home in the afternoon sunshine. "I hope your mum will like the scarf I bought for her. What's for tea, do you think?"

It's now or never, Polly decided.

"Eve?" she said a little hesitantly. "You've been away from home for two days now. Don't you think maybe you should go back?"

Eve was silent. Polly ploughed on.

"Your mum was probably just a bit shocked by your news," she said. "She's had two days to calm down. I'm sure it will be easier to talk to her now. And what about your dad? Don't you miss him?"

Eve's eyes filled with tears. "Of course I miss him. He's the only person at home who loves me for who I am."

"Go home," Polly said gently. "I'll come with you for moral support. We walk past the end of your road on the way back to mine anyway."

Eve swallowed and nodded. "You're right," she said. "I haven't even spoken to Daddy since I left on Friday. I have to go back, don't I?"

They reached Eve's sweeping driveway in five minutes. Two gleaming cars were parked outside the pillared portico of the house. Eve's house always freaked Polly out a little. It felt too big to be allowed.

"Do you want me to come in with you?" Polly asked.

Eve shook her head. "I have to do this by myself. But thank you for everything, Polly. The bed, the vintage stuff. The friendship. I really appreciate it. I'll send Paolo round to pick up my stuff. Oh, and here's your phone." She pressed Polly's phone into her hands. "Don't text Ollie until tomorrow at least," she said sternly. "And give your mum that scarf from me, won't you?"

"Eve!"

Eve's father was hurrying out of the door, taking the steps at the front of the house two at a time. "Evie! You're back. I've been so worried!"

Polly backed away as Eve ran into her father's arms.

She had no place being here. With her father's support through this, Eve would be fine, she knew. It was time to go home. Her room – and bathroom – were her own again. She felt giddy with happiness. Eve was back home, she would have her room to herself again . . . and she had a date with Ollie!

FIFTEEN

The Heartside High football pitches were up on the cliffs above the town. On a fine day, the views were astonishing, and enough to make anyone take their eyes off the football. On a cold day like today, the wind whistled in like a knife. It was starting to give Polly earache.

She shivered, and tried to get comfortable on the long hard benches that ranged along one side of the pitch. She'd chosen her clothes carefully that morning, spending ages changing in the toilets after school. Her outfit felt strange – close-fitting, a bit revealing – but she blended in with the other football groupies on the bench for a change.

Ollie was in the middle of the field with a group of

fifteen other boys, running up and down, his red and black football strip billowing in the wind.

He had never looked so gorgeous. Polly lost herself in admiring his long muscular legs and the way his thick blond hair had whipped itself into an effortless bedhead look that most guys spent hours in front of the bathroom mirror to achieve. His blue eyes sparkled, and he smiled happily, seeming to love every moment. Polly kept pinching herself in the knowledge that Ollie *liked* her. It seemed to defy the laws of nature, somehow.

The game was flowing and the forwards ran up and down in a practised line, although the wind was doing some crazy things to the ball. Polly sifted through her brains for some of the football facts she'd read on the sports page on the back of her mum's newspaper that morning, so she would have them on the tip of her tongue when Ollie came over. She adjusted her pink miniskirt, trying to keep warm in the wind.

"He's so *hot*," someone sighed a little further down the bench. "I can't believe he's single right now."

Polly glanced sideways, to see Megan Moore resting her chin in her hands, her dark heavily made-up eyes following Ollie's every move. Megan was in year nine, the year below Polly and her friends.

"You should go after him, Megan," said Julianne, one of Megan's friends. "You two would look so great together."

Megan swept her long dark hair out of her eyes. "Maybe," she said. She gave a sudden gasp. "Look, he's got the ball again!"

Polly's insides felt like someone was tying knots in them. Megan Moore was after Ollie. Megan was beautiful. How was she supposed to compete?

Ollie likes you, she reminded herself.

She clasped her phone tightly, thinking about the texts she and Ollie had exchanged today. Dozens of them, all flirtatious and full of promise. What did Megan know about that?

She tried to concentrate more on the football. Ollie and the other players were all at the other end of the pitch now, which was confusing her. She could have sworn Ollie had been aiming at the other goal a moment ago.

"Ollie's so dreamy," Megan sighed again.

"He's totally fit," agreed Julianne.

"Sexy," said Tanya, sitting on Megan's other side.

The three of them fell about laughing.

Don't Megan and her friends talk about anything else? Polly thought with some irritation. It was as if the rest of the world didn't exist at all. It was all boys, boys, boys. No art, no politics, no literature. No ambition for the future, beyond perhaps marrying a footballer. Megan and her friends probably didn't even know the name of the prime minister. It was all deeply depressing. Polly wondered what on earth she was doing, sitting here on a freezing bench with such a vapid bunch of people. She felt like a completely different species to them.

The wind was really hurting her ears now. She hunched her head a little further down inside her coat and tried to focus on Ollie. She was here for *him*. No one else.

She suddenly sat up, the pain in her ears forgotten, as a familiar figure headed towards her. Lila's glossy brown hair was pulled back into a tight ponytail, her school skirt rolled up to show her long legs.

Intelligent company at last!

Polly rose to her feet and waved. "Lila! Over here!"

Lila didn't seem to see Polly. She kept walking, her hands deep in her blazer pockets, towards a group of footballers lounging on the sidelines. Polly just had time to register how much make-up Lila was wearing before her friend ran into the arms of a burly football player. They started snogging, to whoops and catcalls from the player's mates.

Polly had never seen Lila even *talking* to this guy before, let alone kissing him. Who was he? What was going on? She wondered uneasily if the make-up she had put on in her attempt to fit in with the other girls made her look as over the top as Lila.

"Lila Murray will kiss anything," said Megan Moore.

"I saw her with another player last week," said Tanya, a gossipy gleam in her eye. "That Liam guy. They were practically eating each other. It was gross."

"Ever since she broke up with Ollie and then Ryan died, she's been snogging anything that moves," Julianne agreed.

Polly felt anxious. Lila had stopped kissing her football guy and was now flirting with his friends. What was going on? She had an uncomfortable

124

memory of Lila telling them all on the beach that she was going "to live like there was no tomorrow". There had been bad times for Lila when she'd lived in London, Polly knew, though she suspected she didn't know the whole story. She'd thought her friend had put all that behind her, but the evidence before her eyes told a different story.

Lila was heading for trouble.

Megan and her friends were still giggling and gossiping. Polly knew she couldn't just sit here and let them bad-mouth Lila. She had to say something.

Before she could open her mouth, the atmosphere suddenly changed. Megan, Julianne and Tanya sat up like meerkats in the African desert as the final whistle blew. The players high-fived each other and headed for the benches.

"Ollie's coming," Julianne hissed in excitement.

Megan and her friends scrambled out of the benches and stood on the sidelines as Ollie approached, football under his arm. Within moments, he was surrounded.

"You were brilliant, Ollie!" Megan said warmly. "I can't believe you scored from that corner!"

What corner? Polly wondered. She hadn't noticed

any corners. She stood up, tugging down her pink skirt, her heart hammering in her chest.

"You could score anywhere," sighed Julianne.

"And you're so hot," murmured Tanya, placing a bold hand on Ollie's sweaty football top. "You're steaming like a racehorse."

Ollie's eyes were sparkling from the exercise. He smiled at them all, still slightly out of breath.

"Hey, girls. Megan, can I talk to you?" Ollie pulled Megan aside and whispered something in her ear. Polly stiffened as Megan whispered something back. What were they talking about?

Paranoia filled her from tip to toe. Her mind rushed through a hundred reasons for Ollie and Megan's cosy little chat, and all of them were bad. Ollie was arranging to meet Megan right after practice! He'd been secretly dating Megan already for weeks! He. . .

Ollie let go of Megan and pushed his way past her to stand in front of Polly's bench.

"Hey!" he said, beaming up at her.

Polly's stomach turned to liquid. He had never looked more gorgeous. She was utterly confused.

"Hey yourself," she managed. "Nice shorts."

Polly cringed internally. *Nice shorts?* Her brain may have been scrambled with thoughts about Megan Moore, but that was no excuse. What was she *thinking?*

Ollie looked down at his worn football shorts. "What, these?" He scrambled over the benches and pulled Polly into a hot, sweaty hug, kissing her soundly on the cheek. "I'm so glad you came," he said. "What did you think of practice?"

Polly was reeling from the heat and warmth of his body. He felt so strong when he put his arms round her. Did he mean it, or was he just the world's most accomplished flirt?

"Pretty good," she said. "I especially liked the bit when you hit the ball."

Ollie shouted with laughter. "We tend to *kick* the ball in football," he said, grinning down at her. "It's a technical term, I know. You'll get the hang of it eventually."

Polly cursed herself for such a basic mistake. She had to get this conversation back on the right track.

"I support Chelsea United," she said brightly. "Did I ever tell you that?"

"Chelsea," Ollie corrected. "Not United."

"The players are really hot," Polly ploughed on. "Like you."

Urgh. That sounded wrong.

Ollie looked puzzled. "Are you winding me up?"

"It must be amazing to sign for a big club," Polly continued doggedly. "You'd have all the money you could ever want."

"Since when were you impressed by footballers?"

Polly smiled awkwardly up at him. She felt like she was dying inside. This was going terribly. It wasn't her at all – what was she thinking, trying to talk about football? What *had* Ollie been talking about with Megan?

"It's a recent interest," she mumbled.

Ollie stared down at her. He seemed about to say something, then apparently changed his mind. "Let's go," he said.

Ollie led her through the benches. Megan, Julianne and Tanya watched in disbelief as Ollie slid his warm palm into Polly's cold one, lifted her hand to his lips and kissed the tips of her fingers.

"I can't believe Ollie's with *Polly Nelson*," said Megan in a hiss, just loud enough for Polly to hear.

"She's a total geek," said Tanya. "Did you hear that stupid comment she made about *hitting* the football?"

"He's totally out of her league," Julianne agreed.

Polly faltered, loosening her grip on Ollie's hand.

Were they right? She was trying so hard to fit in with Ollie's interests, but was she setting herself up for heartbreak? Were she and Ollie destined to fail before they'd even begun?

"What were you and Megan talking about just now?" she said, trying to sound casual.

Ollie shrugged. "Nothing special."

Polly noticed how his eyes flickered. He was lying.

SIXTEEN

Polly thought long and hard about her and Ollie over the next couple of days. The comments from the football groupies on Monday had hurt, and she wasn't sure she trusted Ollie about Megan at all. She'd read a few more magazines and even watched a match on TV so she could say something a bit more intelligent next time Ollie tried to have a conversation about his beloved sport, but it had left her feeling flat and depressed and more convinced of her inadequacy than ever.

She would abandon the football research and focus on her make-up and clothes instead. She hated feeling so small and scruffy next to the other girls with their long legs and perfect shiny hair. Normally she loved her eclectic style and took pride in looking different than all the football clones, but hanging out with Ollie made her feel self-conscious about it.

On Wednesday, she decided to take a risk. She would do her outfit and make-up like she had for the football practice, but she would then take Ollie to do something *she* liked to do. It was all about compromise, right? Maybe she and Ollie could meet halfway.

They had arranged to meet at the end of school on Wednesday. Ollie was standing impatiently at the bottom of the steps as Polly ran to meet him, her bag bouncing on her back. Her short pink skirt still felt weird, but she was getting used to it.

He hugged her tightly, and Polly revelled in the feeling of his arms around her. Despite all her worries, just being around Ollie made her heart beat faster. They still hadn't kissed. Polly found herself looking forward to the prospect more and more.

"So," Ollie said, releasing her but holding tightly on to her hand. "What's the plan?"

"I'm taking you to an art gallery," Polly said.

Ollie looked a little dismayed. "A what?"

Stick with it, Polly told herself.

"An art gallery," she said patiently. "You know, a place where they hang paintings on the wall for people to look at."

"I know what an art gallery is," Ollie said. "I just don't get why we're going there. Don't you have to be really quiet when you go in places like that?"

Polly resisted the urge to roll her eyes. "It's not a library, Ollie. It's a place where people look at beautiful things and then talk about them."

"I'm looking at a beautiful thing right now," said Ollie, gazing into her eyes.

Polly could feel herself melting. Ollie was impossible to resist when he put on the charm.

"Come on," she said, tugging on Ollie's hand. "It's just across town."

"It's not modern art, is it?" he said suspiciously. "That stuff looks like a toddler has just spilt paint and trodden in it."

Polly forced a laugh. "There's a bit more to it than that. Rhi's dad works at a local gallery called the Periwinkle in the Old Town. The gallery supports local artists, which is really important. I often go there for inspiration when I'm designing or customizing something. They have the most amazing stuff."

"Does it have a decent café?" said Ollie. "I'm starving."

Boys and their stomachs, Polly thought with a sigh.

She let Ollie swerve sideways into the newsagent on the way to the Periwinkle. He came out with an armful of crisps.

"Is it much further?" he said, crunching loudly.

"It's right here," she said, and pointed.

The Periwinkle had sky-blue window frames. Three large paintings occupied the window: seascapes, created in whirls of thick oil paint. Polly stood at the window for a moment, savouring the artist's textures. You could almost taste the whirling, grinding sea just by looking.

"What did I tell you?" said Ollie. "Toddler art."

Polly bit her lip. "Hey, come on, be serious for once," she said lightly. She really wished Ollie would ease up on the jokes. This place was important to her. Just as important as the football field was to Ollie. She was making an *effort*. Why couldn't he?

"Polly!" exclaimed Mr Wills, looking round from

where he was hanging a driftwood sculpture on the wall. "Good to see you. Who's your friend?"

"Hi, Mr Wills," said Polly. "This is Ollie. I've brought him to see some paintings."

"Great!" Mr Wills exclaimed. "Are you into art, Ollie?"

Polly prayed Ollie wouldn't say anything stupid. Mr Wills took his job in the gallery very seriously, and painted in his spare time. He was the last person in the world to understand and accept Ollie's quips for what they were: a way of dealing with unfamiliarity.

"I'm more into football, if I'm honest," said Ollie.

Mr Wills spread his hands in acceptance. "It's a free world. Go ahead, Polly. We're pretty quiet today."

"And I can see why," Ollie said in a low voice, staring dubiously at the driftwood sculpture on the wall.

Polly dragged him through to the back of the gallery, to her favourite artist in the world. She felt ridiculously nervous. What would Ollie think? Did it matter what he thought?

"Kazuhiro Mori," said Ollie, reading the name underneath the painting. He turned to Polly in surprise. "I thought you said this was a local artists' gig?"

"Kazuhiro Mori *is* local," Polly explained patiently. "He's been in Heartside Bay for twenty years. He has a really unusual vision."

"You're telling me," said Ollie, looking around.

Polly was determined not to give up. "He's a landscape artist, but not in the traditional sense," she said. "He takes a view and breaks it down into its component parts. Lines and colours."

"OK," said Ollie. He had his concentrating face on.

"This one, for example," Polly said, pointing at a picture that resembled a pile of brightly coloured matchsticks that had spilled haphazardly across a white floor. "Blue for the sea. Red for the roofs. Yellow for the sand. White for the cliffs. Landscapes are basically lines and colours, Ollie. Kazuhiro Mori takes that literally."

She hadn't done a very good job at explaining the painting's appeal, she realized. It was hard to explain why she loved Kazuhiro Mori's paintings of Heartside Bay so much. It was because he saw *through* everything. To the heart of everything. To what was real.

"OK, so I'd maybe have that one on a duvet cover,"

Ollie said, staring at the painting. "I think I can see the sea, maybe. Yeah, and the roofs too!"

Polly felt encouraged. "Exactly! It's really simple, but wonderful."

Ollie sat down on the padded leather bench in the middle of the gallery. "I still don't totally get it," he admitted. "But I think I understand why *you* like it. You like to get to the bottom of things."

"I suppose I do," Polly said, feeling a little surprised at Ollie's flash of insight.

Ollie waved at the pictures. "How do you think this guy would paint a football match?"

It was an interesting question. Polly sat down next to him and thought hard about her answer.

"Circles," she said at last. "The ball and some of the markings on the pitch are circular, right?"

"Have you ever tried kicking a square ball?" Ollie enquired, grinning.

"There'd be squares too, and angles," said Polly, warming to the theme. "The goal posts, the other markings."

"Lots of green?" Ollie said. "For the pitch?"

"Maybe, but. . ." Polly shook her head. "Green

breaks down to the component parts of blue and yellow. He'd do it that way, I think."

She realized that Ollie was looking intently at her.

"What?" she said, blushing.

"You find beauty and significance in everything, don't you?" he said.

His eyes flicked to her mouth. Polly's throat went dry. Was he going to kiss her now?

"Aren't you cold in that?" he said, pointing at her skirt.

Polly flushed bright red. "No," she lied. She tugged at the hem.

"It's not what you usually wear."

"Do you like it?" she asked, with a smile.

Ollie made a face. "Not much."

Polly felt like he'd slapped her. "W . . . what?" she managed. "You think it doesn't look good on me?"

"That's not what I meant," Ollie said. "It's just . . . not really you. Is it?"

Polly felt utterly humiliated. She obviously looked like a prize idiot.

"Anything else wrong with me?" she demanded angrily.

Ollie fiddled with his earlobe. "Now you come to mention it, what's with the big black eyes?"

Polly felt like bursting into tears on the spot.

"I think I'm going to go home," she said abruptly, and quickly turned out of the gallery. Why was everything she did so wrong? Why did it come so easily to everyone else and she couldn't even put on eyeliner without it looking stupid?

Ollie followed. "Polly, I didn't mean to upset you. I just . . . you asked me and I gave you an honest answer. Honesty's good, isn't it? I thought . . . I thought that's what you wanted. Being more honest, not joking all the time. . ." He trailed off.

"It's fine, OK?" Polly said, walking as fast as she could. "I'll see you at school tomorrow."

Ollie was looking worried now, jogging beside her to keep up. "We're still going on that date on Friday, right?"

Polly spun round. "What were you talking to Megan Moore about on Monday?"

Ollie looked startled. "What are you bringing that up for?"

"Tell me!"

"I was asking her if she knew of any good places in town where I could take you on our date on Friday, OK? And she said there was a new Italian place down by the harbour," Ollie said. "So much for the surprise. Happy now?"

Polly didn't say anything. Her head was spinning.

"I think Megan was kind of hoping I'd ask her there instead of you," Ollie added.

"Were you hoping that too?" Polly asked in a trembling voice.

"No!" Ollie protested. "I don't like Megan. I like you. Aren't you listening to me? I've booked a table for you and me on Friday. Or are you going to turn me down again?"

Polly took a deep breath. "I can't do Friday, Ollie," she said. "I'm going to the Funky Fox Festival with Eve and the others."

"But I thought we arranged—"

She was about to cry. All those years she had wanted to be with Ollie, and now that she was actually getting the chance it seemed like nothing was going right.

She fled.

SEVENTEEN

The rest of the week was difficult. Ollie was avoiding her. Polly was sure of it.

There had been plenty of chances for conversation. She and Ollie took most of the same classes. But every time she'd looked for him, he had been among his friends, talking or laughing or looking at his phone. He hadn't glanced up at her once. He hadn't even texted her.

And that's fine by me, Polly thought through gritted teeth. She never wanted to feel that level of humiliation again.

"Penny for them?" said Rhi as the bell went for the end of school on Friday and they gathered at the lockers.

"They're not worth that much," Polly muttered.

"She's mooning over Ollie," said Eve, flipping her hair briskly over her shoulders. "You have to snap out of it, Polly. Boys find mooners *such* a bore."

I've definitely blown it, Polly thought sadly.

Why hadn't she just gone out with Ollie the first time he asked? OK, so Eve had turned up unannounced that night. But that wasn't Polly's problem, was it? Then there'd been the fiasco at Saturday's wedding, and the girls making eyes at Ollie during football practice. The final nail in the coffin had definitely been the art gallery.

This was all her own fault.

Polly wondered if she'd subconsciously sabotaged her own chances with Ollie. She'd been in love with him for so long, maybe on some level she couldn't bear the thought of it not working out between them, and had done everything in her power to stop it from happening at all. The knowledge did nothing to make her feel better about the clothes and make-up disaster.

Eve paled and gripped her locker door as a wave of year eleven boys swept past. One of them looked over his shoulder with a knowing gleam in his eye.

"I'll cure you, babe," he said.

"You might cure rabies," said Eve, looking at the boy like he was dirt on her shoe. "But you won't cure me."

The year eleven boy reddened. "Dumb lesbian," he snarled.

Rhi patted Eve tentatively on the shoulder as his friends dragged him away and out of sight down the corridor. "Are you OK?"

"What do you think?" Eve snapped.

Rhi raised her hands. "I don't want a fight," she said.

Eve's shoulders slumped. She passed a hand over her eyes. "Sorry, Rhi, I didn't mean to bite your head off. It's just – I've had it with all the comments this week. It's very strange for me, you know?"

Her lip wobbled as she turned back to her locker, pulling out her weekend bag with a little more force than necessary.

Being an outcast instead of a queen, Polly thought. Eve would never have experienced anything like this before. It was all very character-building, her mother would have said. But no fun at all.

She pulled herself out of her Ollie gloom. "What an idiot," she said aloud. "Forget him, Eve."

Eve straightened her shoulders. "You're right. I'm not letting some little rat spoil this weekend."

"Funky Fox, here we come!" Lila hooted, and banged hard on the lockers with her fists. Rhi jumped about a mile in the air at the noise.

"Lila," Polly warned, as a teacher put his head out of the classroom door and frowned at them.

"Don't make that face at me, Polly." Lila pulled a mascara wand from her blazer pocket and added a long lick of shiny black mascara to her already heavily mascaraed eyes. "You're not my dad."

Polly sighed. Lila still hadn't explained about the bartender, or her recent string of footballer conquests. She was in her "girls just want to have fun" mode, and there was no reasoning with her. Polly really hoped Lila wouldn't get into any trouble this weekend. Anything could happen at a festival. She was starting to wonder what she'd got herself into.

"Right," said Eve, shouldering her large, brand-new rucksack with some difficulty. "How do we call the bus?"

Rhi giggled. "You can't just call it like a taxi, Eve. We have to get to the bus station and wait."

"What kind of arrangement is that?" Eve demanded. "I wish you'd let me call Paulo. He could get us there in less than an hour."

"That's cheating," said Lila, shouldering her own infinitely scruffier bag. "You won't get into the festie vibe, Eve. Besides, we might meet some cute guys on the bus."

Rhi clapped her hands with excitement. "This is going to be such an awesome weekend. I can't believe we're going to see Polarize live!" She started humming a Polarize track, one that had been playing on the radio for weeks.

"Harry Lawson is *hot*," Lila giggled, humming along as they walked out of school and into the bright afternoon light. "I might hang around backstage and see if I can get his number."

The sun was setting as the four girls struggled through the farm gate. Polly's rucksack straps were biting into her shoulders and her feet were wet. She hadn't banked on trudging two miles from the bus stop to get to this point. She thought longingly of her cosy bed. She wouldn't be seeing it for two whole nights. Already, that was feeling like a lifetime.

"Whew!" Eve wiped her forehead. "This festival had better be as good as everyone says. I haven't walked that far since our ski lift broke down in Chamonix."

Polly found herself looking down at a great field full of people. Tents were already crammed in, forming brightly coloured lines down the hillside. Pennants fluttered from the bigger marquees, and there was a smell of barbecue in the air. Way down at the bottom of the field stood the main stage with its distinctive, point-eared Funky Fox canopy. The more she stared at the scene, the harder she was finding it to breathe. It was *massive*. She had no idea the festival would be this big, or this crowded.

"I can't believe we're here," said Rhi in excitement, surveying the scene.

Lila whooped.

Polly concentrated on not being sick. The anxiety was creeping up on her in familiar, nagging waves. There was no running water or proper toilets. The crowd was getting bigger by the minute, multiplying like some horrible kind of virus. She gritted her teeth.

I'm stuck here for forty-eight hours, she thought in horror. *And there's nothing I can do about it.*

"Our pitch is over there," said Eve, pointing towards the sunnier side of the field. "Not too close to the stage, so we can get some sleep."

"I'm not sleeping," Lila announced. "Not with all the fun I plan to have."

Rhi had brought the tent.

"That is *awesome*!" Polly gasped as Rhi unfurled it proudly. "Where did you get it?"

"I saved up for it, and asked for the rest for Christmas," Rhi said proudly. "I've been dying to use it ever since I got it. Isn't it the most gorgeous thing you've ever seen?"

People started to gather, looking and pointing. The tent looked exactly like an old-style camper van, complete with yellow and white walls and split-screen-style plastic windows. When it was pegged into place, it looked even more realistic.

"I love it," Polly gasped as they went inside with

their rucksacks. She'd almost forgotten her nerves in the wonder of putting up such a brilliant tent.

"It's very cosy, Rhi," said Eve in approval. She laid out her bedroll and sleeping bag and checked her watch. "Now, there's no time to waste. We have an appointment."

"Too right," Lila said, slinging her rucksack down. "We have an appointment with *fun*. And I don't want to be late. Who's with me?"

Eve raised a finger. "We'll have the fun *after* the appointment."

"What are you talking about, Eve?" asked Polly in confusion.

Eve's eyes gleamed. "I have a surprise for Rhi," she said. "An audition in one of the tents."

Lila shrieked, putting her hands to her mouth. Polly watched as Rhi turned a delicate shade of green.

"What?" Rhi squeaked.

"It's an *X Factor*-style competition they're holding near the main stage," Eve explained happily. "I called them and booked you in. Come on, we've only got fifteen minutes to get there."

147

EIGHTEEN

"I don't *want* to audition," Rhi bleated.

They stood outside the tent in a pool of sunshine beside the main stage, alongside a group of other singers all trilling and practising their moves. AUDITIONS was written in thick, slanting chalk pen on a blackboard outside the tent flaps. YOU THINK YOU CAN SING? PROVE IT AND WIN THE CHANCE TO SING LIVE TO THE CROWDS ON THE FUNKY FOX MAIN STAGE SATURDAY 4 P.M.

Rhi was holding so tightly to Polly's hand, Polly was losing all circulation in her fingers. "Don't make me do this," Rhi moaned. "I can't believe you set this up without telling me!"

"Maybe it's not such a good idea, Eve," said Lila.

She caught the eye of a tall boy with long blond dreads behind them in the queue, and gave him a flirty little wave. "Remember what happened last time you tried to steer Rhi's music career."

"Exactly!" said Rhi.

"That was different," Eve said. "I was a different person then. And anyway, Rhi, you said you appreciated the experience. These people want original songs. Not covers, or dance tracks that don't suit your voice. That means you can sing one of your own songs."

The queue shuffled forward.

"Maybe you should give it a go," Polly said, keen to encourage Rhi. She did have the most wonderful voice. "You said you'd been working on some new material with Brody?"

"They won't want to hear that," said Rhi in a small voice. "Besides, I need Brody with me to sing it."

"Rhi, I thought you were serious about your music career," Eve said impatiently. "You have to take opportunities like this whenever they come along."

They were inside the tent now. The girl on the stage was singing badly, Polly realized – flat and hopelessly out of time. The three judges at the back of the tent were conferring and shaking their heads.

"If that's the competition," she coaxed, "you could really ace this."

Rhi was weakening. "I don't have my guitar!" she said in a last-minute bid to avoid the inevitable.

"That's OK," said Lila. She flashed a sideways look at the guy with dreads. "This little hottie behind us is going to lend us his. Aren't you?"

Dreads looked a little dazed by the full force of Lila's attention. "I am?"

Lila pressed a kiss on his cheek. "Of course you are," she said, squeezing his arm and laughing up at him. "And maybe we could meet up later? As a thank-you."

Polly yanked Lila away. "Eve organized this weekend especially for us to have some proper girl time," she said in a low voice. "Can you please stop thinking about boys for just two days?"

"You're such a spoilsport, Polly," Lila grumbled.

Dreads lent Rhi his guitar.

Rhi looked more composed now she had a guitar in her hands, and climbed on the stage without too much prodding from the others. She played hesitantly at first, unfamiliar with the instrument around her neck. Polly leaned her head on Lila's shoulder and listened as Rhi built her way into one of Polly's favourite songs: "Way Down Low".

"Way down low, deep in our canyon of gold," Rhi sang. "Way to go, let all your stories unfold. . ."

Polly eyed the judges. She wasn't even sure they were listening. It was such a great song. Rhi had true talent.

"Way to go," Rhi sang, strumming the guitar one last time. "Way . . . down . . . low."

Polly, Eve and Lila clapped hard. Behind them, Dreads and a few others were clapping too.

"Thanks," said the head judge in a bored voice.

"Yeah, cheers," said the second judge, picking his fingernails.

"Thanks for coming," said the third judge. "Next!"

Rhi climbed off the stage and handed Dreads his guitar. Polly felt gutted for her. It looked like the judges hated her music.

"Is that all you can say?" Eve said indignantly to the judges. "Don't you even have an opinion? Clearly you weren't even listening. My friend has the best voice I've ever heard."

"We don't give feedback," said the head judge. "If we gave feedback to everyone we heard, we'd be here until Wednesday."

"Can we go?" Rhi muttered.

"Come on, Eve," said Polly, taking Eve's arm. "They aren't interested."

Eve shook Polly off. "Seriously," she said to the judges, "you all need your hearing tested. You wouldn't know talent if it kicked you up the—"

"We're going now," Lila interrupted loudly. "Rhi wants to get out of here and I don't blame her. Polarize are on the main stage at any minute."

Grumbling, Eve let the others pull her out of the auditions tent to take up decent positions near the main stage. "What a bunch of amateurs," she complained. "I'm sorry we even bothered."

"I'm not," said Rhi unexpectedly. "It was good for me to get up there and sing. I enjoyed it."

"Never mind," Polly said, giving Rhi an encouraging cuddle. "There'll be other chances."

There was a wail of feedback. Lila let out a massive

scream that almost ruptured Polly's eardrums as Harry Lawson moved across the stage like a lazy panther, followed by his bandmates: three skinny guys in even skinnier jeans. Polarize, live and in the flesh, for the first of two sets they were doing over the Funky Fox weekend. Right under their noses.

The band kicked off with their hit "Awake and Aware". As the familiar opening riff kicked in, Polly forgot all her worries and anxieties. The press of the crowd, the flashing lights, the ringing in her head – none of it mattered. It was just her and her friends and the music, all mashed up together. Nothing else.

Three bands and four orders of chips later, they headed back to their campsite, happy and exhausted.

"Polarize smashed it," said Lila. She was still pumped from the music and jumping from side to side. "Best set of the night, don't you think? We have to see them tomorrow too if we can."

"Mental Element were good too," said Eve. "I didn't rate that rapper guy though."

"DJ Tux is a legend," protested Lila. "But he wasn't on best form tonight, I have to agree. I think the amps were playing up."

It was hard to see where they were going in the dark. A few campfires flickered, showing them the way towards the place where they'd last seen their tent.

"Are we sure this is the right campsite?" said Lila, looking around the sea of canvas and campfires.

"I can't see the tent anywhere," Eve said. She sounded worried. "You'd think it was too distinctive to lose, wouldn't you?"

Polly's gaze settled on a strange, empty-looking pitch. She recognized the red tent on the left, and the pennants that fluttered from a tent a little further down the field. Her heart sank.

"It was there," she said, pointing. "Wasn't it?"

The others gaped. Rhi let out a wail of misery.

The camper-van tent and all their belongings had apparently vanished off the face of the earth, without leaving a trace.

NINETEEN

Polly opened her eyes. She was lying face down on a patch of damp moss with blades of grass sticking to her cheek. Was someone calling her name?

She sat up blearily, dislodging a shower of dew from the blanket over her legs. Every part of her ached.

Eve, Rhi and Lila were still asleep beside her, curled up together like puppies in a basket beneath the blankets they had bummed from a couple of other festival-goers. This top part of the field was the driest, most sheltered part they had been able to find that wasn't covered in tents. It had a gorgeous view right down the valley but it was miles from anywhere. Who could be calling her way out here?

Polly rubbed her eyes, dislodging mud and grit.

What a night. An hour at festival security, reporting the theft, had got them nowhere. No one seemed to care. They hadn't even been given a cup of tea to keep them warm. It had been way too late to go home by the time they admitted defeat. So here they were. Sleeping in the middle of a field, like damp cows.

Rhi had slept particularly badly, dissolving into tears over the loss of her tent every few minutes. It had been rough, losing something she was so proud of the very first time it had been used. And their *rucksacks*. Polly groaned at the memory. Clothes, make-up, fresh underwear. Toothpaste.

Running her tongue tentatively over her furry-feeling teeth, she cupped her hands and blew into them.

Urgh, she thought, wrinkling her nose. *Dog breath on top of everything else.*

She checked her watch. It was nearly noon, she realized with some horror. She was desperate for a shower, but there was no chance of that.

"RHI? LILA? EVE? POLLY?"

Polly's heart lurched. She recognized that voice. But it couldn't be.

Could it?

Squinting into the sun, she stood up and gazed down the field in disbelief. Three familiar figures were jogging towards them, dodging guy ropes and sleeping bags. The blond guy in the middle was raising his hand and waving.

"POLLY!" Ollie shouted again, waving hard.

Polly shook Lila. "Wake up!" she said frantically. "It's Ollie, Max and Josh!"

Lila's hair was a mess, wild and tangled and sweaty from all the moshing around the main stage the night before. "What?" she squeaked, sitting bolt upright. Mascara streaked down her face like wet spiders' legs. "Josh is here? Like, *here*?"

Polly pointed wordlessly down the field. Her brain was whizzing at a hundred miles an hour. *I look like a nightmare*, she thought in despair. Her hair, her clothes . . . her *breath*! Of all the times to see Ollie. . .

Rhi and Eve sat up, yawning.

"What's going on?" Eve mumbled.

"Ollie, Max and Josh are coming towards us," Polly repeated. This couldn't be happening. "How did they find us?"

Rhi raised her hand. "That was me," she confessed.

"I hit a really low patch at about four when you guys were asleep. So I climbed one of the trees over there to get reception and called Max."

Eve clapped her hands to her face. "I look like a scarecrow," she gasped.

"We all do," said Polly. What had Rhi been thinking of? Didn't she realize how embarrassing this would be?

"Look on the bright side, guys," said Lila. "They've got stuff with them."

"Found you!" Ollie exclaimed, reaching them at last. He looked around at the group, but avoided glancing directly at Polly. "We've been searching all over this place." He dumped his rucksack on the grass and looked at their makeshift campsite. "You slept out here all night?"

"'Slept' is overstating things." Eve yawned, covering her hand with her mouth. "Do you have any food?"

Josh opened the flap on his rucksack and pulled out four fresh baguettes. Apples came next, followed by a pot of jam and a large Thermos of coffee.

"Call the Three Amigos," he said, spreading out the food on the damp grass with a flourish. "We deliver anywhere. Even to the top of a field."

Polly couldn't bring herself to look at Ollie. What was he doing here? She'd thought he had given up on her. But if he had come all this way, surely it meant he wanted to try again. But he wouldn't even look directly at her. She was so confused. She sank her teeth into a baguette, hoping the bread might absorb some of her bad breath. Eve grabbed an apple. Rhi and Lila both lunged for the Thermos.

"You guys are angels," said Lila, her hands wrapped possessively around a plastic mug of hot black coffee. "I can't believe you brought all this. This coffee's like *nectar* – last night was the worst."

"We've come for the girls' weekend." Looking pleased with himself, Max sat beside Rhi and planted a loud kiss on her muddy cheek. He managed to spill her coffee down her front, making her yelp. "I know we're not girls, but I'm guessing that's OK. Right, Rhi?"

Polly allowed herself an inward sigh. Max may have been good-looking, but he really was the most annoying guy at Heartside High.

"Thanks, Max," said Rhi, mopping at her top.

"It was nothing," said Max with a wink. "But don't

forget to thank me every day for the next six months. Can I have half your baguette?"

Polly hunched over her baguette and watched out of the corner of her eye as Ollie and Josh put up the tents. She admired the way Ollie's muscular arms flexed as he yanked on the tent ropes and joked around with Josh. Josh was looking as cute as ever, a trendy hat perched on his head and his long legs encased in slim-fitting green jeans. Glancing across, Polly noted how thoughtfully Lila was looking at Josh. There was hope for those two yet, she decided.

"Whew," said Ollie, wiping his forehead. "Tents are done. Thanks for your help, Max."

Lying prone on the rug next to Rhi with his mouth full of baguette crumbs, Max raised a lazy hand in acknowledgement.

Ollie and Josh had arranged the tents in such a way that they formed a cosy semi-circle around everyone. Polly sat curled up on her damp rug in the middle, her belly full of bread and apples and her spirit calm and contented. She would have kissed Ollie in gratitude if her breath hadn't been so bad.

"This is for you." It was the first time Ollie had

spoken to her directly since the disastrous end to their date at the gallery.

Polly looked up. Ollie was waving a little bag at her.

"Oh my gosh," she gasped, grabbing it and looking inside. Deodorant. Toothbrushes. And toothpaste. "Ollie, you're a genius!"

Ollie smiled. "I figured girls need stuff like this. Right?"

"You don't know how right," said Polly, clutching the little bag to her chest.

She smiled a little nervously back at him. Was he still mad at her for cancelling their date? She wished she hadn't shouted at him the way she did.

Ollie leaned in closer. Polly squeaked and put her hands over her mouth. Her breath still reeked. If he came any nearer, he'd probably faint with disgust.

"You still owe me that kiss," he said.

Polly felt a little surge of hope.

"But we need to talk, Polly," he added quietly. "You have to make up your mind. Do you want to make room in your life for me, or not? I can't wait for ever."

TWENTY

After asking the nearest group to watch their tents, the whole group headed into the heart of the festival, in full swing now it was mid-afternoon. They took in some stilt walkers in crazy metal headpieces, and tried the bungee run. Ollie wound up in the thick of a scratch football match among cheering festival-goers near the main stage. Eve had her hands hennaed; Max dragged an unimpressed Rhi over to check out the vintage motorbikes parked in gleaming black and chrome rows by the festival gates.

Polly browsed among the vintage stalls, finding old pieces of lace and gorgeous antique ribbons among the cluttered tables and wondering what she was going to do about Ollie. He'd made it clear something had to change.

Lila and Josh disappeared for an hour, returning triumphantly with two sketches: one Josh had drawn of the view looking down on the Funky Fox main stage, the other a portrait of Lila clenching a daisy between her teeth. Music was everywhere – on the main stage, in several smaller tents ranged around the edge of the farm, drumming groups gathered around the central tent pole with its flapping Funky Fox flag, guitar players by the big lake that gleamed at the bottom of the valley.

Polly soaked up the sounds, the sights and the smells. Most of all, she soaked up the sight of Ollie, joking and laughing with the others. He really did like her. He had proven it over and over. Despite all the mistakes she had made, he kept coming back and trying again. But he had made clear he wouldn't do it for ever. She just had to make a leap and make herself vulnerable. True, she wasn't like all the other girls at school, but Ollie liked her for who she was. She had to believe that. It was when she had been herself– when she had showed Ollie the artwork that had meant so much to her, when they had danced together at the wedding, that she and Ollie really connected. It was only when she tried to dress like the other girls or follow Eve's advice that things went wrong. She had to trust herself. And trust Ollie.

"You guys should have been here last night," said Lila, resting her head on Josh's tummy as they sat companionably around a fire that Ollie had built back at their tents. "We should have invited them to begin with, Eve."

"Excuse me for planning a girls-only weekend," said Eve waspishly.

Max smirked. "Your kind of weekend, hey Eve?"

Polly winced at the grin Max shot in Ollie's direction.

"Shut up, Max," said Rhi.

"It was a joke!" Max protested. "Just because Eve's a lesbian now, doesn't mean she can't take a joke. Does it?"

Eve's eyes were narrowing to slits.

"Who wants food?" Polly said brightly, keen to avert a fight.

Lila groaned and clutched her stomach. "I've eaten a horse today already."

"It was probably a cow," said Josh. "Although I

wouldn't ask that burger van too many questions."

"It really was a great night," Lila sighed.

Josh raised himself on his elbows. "Earlier it was the worst night ever, and now it's the best? That's impossible. Have you ever considered a career in politics, Lila?"

Lila made herself more comfortable. "If I were prime minister, I'd ban school and make festivals compulsory," she said dreamily.

"What useful citizens that would produce," Polly pointed out.

"No lessons at all?" said Max.

"Maybe I'd teach fun," Lila said. "Half the world doesn't know how to have it."

"That's a lesson I'd pay good money to attend," said Ollie.

"Pose for me, Lila?" Josh suggested, pulling out his sketchbook.

Lila arranged herself on the rug, fluffing her hair out. "How's this?"

"Gorgeous," said Josh. Polly could see that he was blushing.

It was great that Josh and Lila were getting along so

well today. After the awkward scene at the wedding, Polly had feared all hope of romance between them had been ruined. Now she wasn't so sure. Josh was just what Lila needed. Calm, steady, kind.

Someone somewhere was playing the guitar. The notes floated in the still afternoon air. Polly closed her eyes, imagining a world where Lila and Josh got together. Where she and Ollie finally kissed each other.

"Stop *pawing* me, Max," Rhi snapped suddenly.

Polly opened one eye to see Max lifting his hands in the air. "I thought boyfriends and girlfriends held hands," he said. "My mistake."

"That wasn't my hand," said Rhi coolly.

"Whatever. You need to chill out, Rhi."

"And *you* need to keep your hands where I can see them!"

Max got up and dusted down his jeans. "I can tell when I'm not wanted," he said a little sourly. "I'm going to get a burger. Anyone joining me?"

Ollie shook his head. Josh was too busy sketching Lila even to reply. Max shrugged and jogged away down the field.

"Max is really getting on my nerves today," Rhi

burst out. "He doesn't know when to stop, you know? I wish I hadn't called him last night."

Polly sat up. "If you hadn't called him, Ollie and Josh wouldn't have come either."

"Good to know we're appreciated," Josh murmured, not looking up from his sketchbook as he drew the outline of Lila's eyes.

"Max is an idiot," said Eve as she admired her hennaed hands. It was the first thing she'd said since Max's misguided crack about her sense of humour. "You're too good for him, Rhi."

Polly felt a fresh prickle of hope. *Lila and Josh getting together* and *Rhi and Max splitting up?* she thought. That would be a dream outcome to this weekend. She wondered briefly if it was bad to wish heartbreak on people. Then she decided Max's heart was probably made of rubber, and unlikely to break at all.

"Everyone could see how much you loved your little motorbike tour," Lila murmured from her position on the rug.

Rhi laughed. "I would have preferred to do the henna thing with Eve. But when Max gets an idea into his head, it's difficult to shift."

Polly glanced a little awkwardly at Ollie.

We shouldn't be talking about his best friend like this, she thought. *Not in front of him.*

"I'm not listening," said Ollie, catching Polly's worried glance. "Girl talk brings me out in a rash. Hey, Max! Wait up!"

"Ollie has a very nice shape," Lila remarked, tilting her head to watch Ollie as he jogged easily down the field after Max.

Polly felt a stab of jealousy deep in her belly. She didn't think she could bear it if Lila got interested in Ollie again.

"I told you not to move your head, Lila," Josh said a little sharply.

Rhi pushed her cloudy hair off her face and sighed. "I'm starting to think you guys are right," she said. "Max isn't the guy for me after all. It's just . . . we've been together for such a long time, and—"

"And he cheated on you," Eve added. "With me."

"I don't need reminding, thanks," said Rhi a little drily. "Let's just say that at times like this, the single life looks . . . very appealing."

It was funny how things could change, Polly thought. One minute Rhi and Max were loved up and she was as far away from dating Ollie as it was possible to be. The next, Rhi was thinking about dumping Max, and Ollie wanted to be with her.

"Come on," said Rhi, getting to her feet as Josh put the finishing touches to his sketch and told Lila she could move. "Let's go see what's going on down by the main stage."

"Ollie and Max might not be able to find us again," said Polly, feeling a little worried. She had to talk to Ollie, to tell him she was ready to try again.

"And that's a bad thing?" Eve enquired. "Good idea, Rhi. I need some music."

The crowds were drifting down the field towards the main stage, as if drawn there by a magnet. There was an energy in the air that Polly wanted to embrace, but she found herself feeling a little freaked out instead. She wished Ollie hadn't disappeared with Max.

A fat raindrop suddenly hit the end of her nose, making her jump. The sky had clouded over, she realized, and ominous grey clouds were rolling in from the west.

"Oops," said Lila, gazing upwards as they flowed on down the hill in the middle of the crowd. "Maybe we should have stayed in our tents after all."

Polly couldn't tear her eyes from the sky. It was almost impossible to believe the speed at which it was rushing from blue to black. A couple of people whooped, lifting their arms to the sky as the rain fell more heavily.

"Boy," said Josh, sheltering his head with his arms. "This stuff is cold."

There was a crack of thunder. Someone behind Polly screamed. The rain was really falling hard now, banging into the ground in long silvery nails, and Polly's feet were starting to slip on the rapidly dampening grass.

I have to get out of here, she thought anxiously. She had the most horrible sensation that the sky was about to fall on her head.

She tried to turn round, but there were too many people. As the sound of the drumming rain grew louder, so did the shouts of the crowd. Polly was being bumped around like a pinball. She could feel a wave of hysteria lapping at her, threatening to overwhelm her. She couldn't see the others.

"Help!" she screamed, whirling around. "Help! I can't . . . I. . ."

Her feet were sliding from beneath her, like an ice skater on a bad day. She hit the ground with a squelch and a sob of panic. Curling her hands over her head, Polly pulled herself into a tiny ball. Feet thundered past her, uncaring, missing her by millimetres. She would die here. . . She would be crushed into the wet earth and drown in the mud. . .

In the depths of her terror, Polly felt a hand grabbing her and pulling her to her feet.

"Up you get," said Ollie. "Are you OK? You went down like a bowling pin."

Dimly Polly knew there was mud all over her clothes, and on her face, and her hair hung round her face in wet black rats' tails. In normal circumstances, she would have run away to avoid Ollie seeing her like this. But right now, he was the sweetest thing she'd ever seen.

"Ollie," Polly sobbed, and clung to him like he was

a life raft.

His arms came round her, protecting her from the press of the muddy, jostling, shouting, screaming, muddy crowd.

"Don't look at me," Polly wept, huddling in closer to him. "I look like a freak."

She felt Ollie's fingers beneath her chin, bringing her gaze up to his.

"You've never looked so beautiful," he said.

It was as if someone had suddenly pressed a mute button. The noise of the crowd faded to nothing. Polly noticed no one pushing, or shoving, or screaming. All she could see were Ollie's blue eyes.

"Oh!"

Someone had rammed right into her, sending her spinning sideways, back down into the mud. Only it wasn't mud this time. It was rubbish. Sweet-smelling takeaway boxes, sticky drink cartons, nameless sludge mushed into the ground.

Panic took full hold, squeezing Polly tightly around the throat. She screamed and screamed until her throat was raw.

"*Urgh!*"

It was in her hair. Vile, stinky goo was dripping down her neck, down the collar of her shirt.

"Polly, it's OK, calm down. . ."

Polly couldn't focus; the feel of the rubbish all over her body made her squirm. Ollie was reaching for her again, but Polly felt hideous. "No!" she shrieked. "Don't touch me!"

She had to do something about the grime. She needed to find a shower. "Please," she said desperately, "I need to go."

And she blundered away, half-blind with horror and shame.

TWENTY-ONE

In the midst of her panic, something made Polly look back over her shoulder.

Ollie stood like a statue amid the running, shouting mayhem. His bright blue eyes had dimmed. He wasn't smiling. His shoulders were slumped and tired, and his whole body radiated with hurt. The rain hammered down unrelentingly, soaking his blond hair flat to his head. He was immobilized, as if his feet were glued to the ground. All around him, the crowd thundered on.

All of this, Polly glimpsed in an instant. She faltered. She couldn't do this to him, not again. She yelled his name. "Ollie!"

Ollie seemed to wake up at her shout. A fresh surge

of something flickered in his gaze. He started to run after her.

"Polly!" he bawled. "Come back!"

"*Polly!*"

Polly tried to turn around but the crowd was stampeding now. She found herself caught up in the middle, running hard in the thick of it all. She wanted to turn back and find Ollie, to apologize for hurting him so badly, but she had no choice but to keep running or risk another fall. She wished the ground would open its great earthy mouth and gulp her down whole. She had run away from him *again*. She had well and truly freaked out back there. She must have looked like a madwoman.

The rain was easing up now, and glimpses of blue sky were creeping into view. A shaft of brilliant sunlight pierced the murk, lighting up the lake and turning it a sheet of beaten silver. Polly realized with a stab of shock that the stampede was heading to the water's edge, an unstoppable force with only one thing in mind.

There was a yell as the first wave of the crowd hit the lake. Spray fountained into the air. People were jumping in everywhere Polly looked, climbing on each other's shoulders, somersaulting like circus tumblers, bombing into the water with their knees up to their chins. Polly thought that she glimpsed Josh and Lila, Eve, Rhi and Max leaping in with their arms aloft. In the next moment her view was obliterated as she reached the lake's grassy edge.

Polly welcomed the freezing blast against her skin as she hit the water feet-first. Ducking down, she swam fast, away from the frenzy to open water. Glorious, clean, cold water. She ducked and rolled and rubbed and ducked again, pulling her hands down the back of her hair. Revelling in the sensation of being clean at last.

She trod water, gasping, her heartbeat slowing to something approaching normal, watching the crowds around her hurling themselves into the water like wild-eyed, muddy lemmings. Her clothes wafted around her in the lake like seaweed.

All around her, people were laughing and hugging in the water. One girl, her face heavily streaked with running make-up, was kissing a boy whose drenched and battered hat sat comically over his eyes. Polly had seen the couple before, dancing to Polarize on Friday night. She'd thought then what a strange pair they were: the glamorous girl with posh accessories and the hippy boy with mismatched socks. Never in a million years would Polly have put them together. Now, wet and gasping with laughter, she could barely tell them apart. They were who they were.

Reaching up, Polly clutched at the silver locket dangling around her neck beneath her blouse. It felt solid and real beneath her fingers.

"POLLY!"

A few metres down the bank, Ollie was still running, waving at her.

"Here!" Polly shouted, releasing the locket and lifting her arms. "I'm over here!"

Ollie spotted her. He hurled himself into the lake, knees clutched tightly against his chest in a great spray of water. Polly struck towards him, splashing and gasping and intent on only one thing.

"Ollie! I'm here! I'm sorry, I'm so sorry!"

Ollie rose out of the water, wet and sleek like a spluttering otter. "Polly, you total nutcase. What did you run away like that for?"

"I'm sorry," Polly repeated. "For everything. I'm sorry for running away. And for not trusting you. And for cancelling our date. And for not responding to your texts." Polly thought of the litany of mistakes she had made. Everything came down to overthinking. For once in her life she just needed to act.

She found that they had reached a shallow part of the lake and she could just touch the bottom with her toes. For a moment she stood and looked at Ollie's questioning face. Then she reached for him, touched the rough wetness of his shirt. Pulled him towards her and kissed him hard on the mouth.

Ollie's arms were around her in a flash, pulling her tightly against him. His lips were soft, but he kissed her hungrily, like he never wanted to stop. Polly couldn't breathe for the fireworks exploding in her belly. At last, she was kissing the boy she had liked for so long. It had been worth every moment of the wait.

"Never run away from me again," Ollie whispered against her lips, his hands stroking her wet hair. "I'm sorry too. I'm sorry I made jokes about the artwork. I'm sorry I got pissed off when you were just trying to help your friends. I'm sorry for being such a fool. I love you, Polly Nelson. I always have and I always will. You mean everything to me. And I will never, ever let you go."

His lips were on hers again, deeper and more searching than ever. Polly softened against him, holding on to every part of him that she could reach, running her fingers through his wet hair and cupping the back of his neck, pulling him harder towards her and kissing, kissing, kissing. Nothing mattered but this. Now.

Just this.

TWENTY-TWO

Polly had no sense of time passing. It was just her and Ollie, in each other's arms. The lake was quieter now, illuminated by bright sunlight as sudden as the storm that had preceded it, as people scrambled ashore, heading off to find somewhere warm to dry off.

"It is just me," said Ollie as the water sloshed around their chests, "or are your feet wet too?"

Giggling, Polly slid her hands away from his shoulders. "We should find the others," she said. "They're probably wondering where we are."

"It's none of their business," said Ollie promptly. "This is one party they aren't invited to."

He pulled her back for a final kiss. Once again Polly lost herself at the feeling of his mouth moving against hers – until her teeth started chattering against his lips.

"Ollie, I'm freezing," she confessed, pulling back reluctantly. "Can we get out of here?"

Ollie looked horrified at the way Polly's teeth were clattering against each other. "I'm sorry, I didn't think. We have to get you out of here and warm you up."

"My heart's warm enough," said Polly, gazing shyly at him. "It's just the rest of me that needs a little work."

Ollie laughed. Hoisting her into his arms, he waded through the water towards the shore. Polly rested her head on his chest, her arms round his neck, quietly content to be there.

"Solid ground, your majesty," said Ollie, putting her down on a stretch of grass in a patch of bright sunlight. It felt wonderful on Polly's chilled limbs. "Now all we need is a towel or a blanket or something. Stay here."

He turned and sprinted away up the field. Polly watched him go, feeling as if she was in a daze. A parallel universe. Ollie and her. Her and Ollie. Together at last.

He was back in minutes, panting and pressing his

hand to his side. "One for you and one for me," he said, wrapping Polly up in one blanket and draping himself in another.

They sat together by the lake, their heads resting together, warming up and drying off. Polly was almost drifting away to sleep when she saw Rhi running towards them, waving. Her hair had mostly dried after the jump in the lake, and it looked like she had been able to change into clean clothes, but for some reason she looked frantic.

"Have you seen Max?"

"Nope," said Ollie, draping his arm more comfortably around Polly's shoulders.

"I've lost him," Rhi wailed. "I have to talk to him and I've lost him."

She shaded her eyes, scouting the field. But it was impossible to pick anyone out in the surging crowds.

"We haven't seen anyone since everyone jumped in the lake," said Polly.

The anxiety fell away from Rhi's face as she grinned. "Good, wasn't it? Eve's annoyed because it ruined her silk top."

"What do you need to find Max for anyway?" Polly

asked.

A loudspeaker hanging in the tree over their heads suddenly squealed into life, making Polly jump so much she landed in Ollie's lap. Ollie captured her and held her there. Polly could see understanding dawning in Rhi's face.

"You finally got it together? That's so cute!"

The loudspeaker crackled. "The results of the Funky Fox talent contest are in!"

Polly had all but forgotten the contest Eve had made Rhi take part in. There was a dim cheer from the crowds.

"And we're pleased to announce that *first* prize goes to . . . Rhiannon Wills."

Rhi let out such a loud scream that people nearby turned and looked at her, pointing and smiling, guessing her identity.

"*Rhi!*" Polly gasped, as what she'd just heard kicked in.

"I didn't think they liked it," Rhi whispered hoarsely with her hands pressed to her face.

Ollie was on his feet, pounding Rhi on the shoulders. "That's fantastic, Rhi. Well done! You won!"

"Oh my gosh!" Polly squealed. Her head felt completely scrambled. "That's amazing! You're amazing! I knew you'd smashed it in there, I knew it!"

"What's the prize?" Ollie asked.

Polly tried to think but she couldn't remember.

"Singing on the main stage," Rhi whispered. "Today. Four o'clock."

Ollie checked his watch. "Damn, the lake stopped it," he said. "What time is it now?"

"Would Rhiannon Wills make her way to the main stage, please," said the loudspeaker. "Rhiannon Wills, main stage."

"I guess it's four o'clock," Polly said.

Rhi sat down abruptly on the grass. "I can't do it."

"Of course you can," Polly coaxed. She pulled Rhi back on to her feet. "You've got loads more experience singing in front of crowds now you've been doing all that wedding singing."

"And your and Brody's gigs at the Heartbeat, don't forget them," Ollie put in.

"I can't do it!" Rhi wailed.

Polly went into action mode. "We need to find that dreadlocked guy with the guitar. Ollie, I think I saw his tent not far from ours. You go and fetch the guitar, OK? Rhi, you and I are going over to the main stage right now."

Ollie hurried away, heading back to their tents again.

"OK," Rhi said, quivering gently. "Polly, you'll stay with me, won't you? I can't do it without you."

Polly pushed Rhi gently towards the stage. "I'm right here," she said. "I'm always here for you, Rhi."

The judges were waiting in the cordoned-off backstage area, walkie-talkies in their hands.

"Rhi, right?" said the head judge. "Good to see you again. Well done for yesterday. Are you ready to go?"

"We're waiting for a guitar," Polly said quickly.

The judge nodded. "Fine. Five minutes. In you go." And he ushered Rhi and Polly into the backstage area.

"Stay calm, Rhi," Polly instructed, guiding Rhi towards the stage steps. "We'll just hang out here until Ollie gets back with that guitar, OK?"

"Which one of you guys won the prize?" said a familiar voice.

Polly's mouth went completely dry. Harry Lawson, lead singer of Polarize, was looking quizzically at her and Rhi through his thick blond fringe. For a horrible moment, Polly didn't think her voice was going to work.

"Her," she managed, jabbing a thumb in the direction of Rhi, who was looking at stunned as Polly was.

"Awesome," said Harry, grinning appreciatively at Rhi. "We'll be listening, yeah?"

Ollie arrived, panting, holding the guitar. He did a double-take.

"You're Harry Lawson," he said stupidly.

"Last time I checked," said Harry. He looked at Rhi again. "Good luck. You're on."

One of the stage managers clipped a mic to Rhi's top. Polly gave Rhi a gentle push between the shoulder blades. "We'll be right here!" she said encouragingly. "Go for it!"

Rhi climbed the steps on to the stage with a tentative glance over her shoulder. Backstage, Ollie pulled Polly into his arms.

"I can't believe I just told Harry Lawson his own name," he mumbled as he hugged Polly and rested his head on the top of hers. Polly laughed softly and hugged him back.

"You weirdo," she said softly, relishing how easy it felt being with Ollie when she stopped overthinking.

They had a good view from where they were standing. Through the wings, Polly could see tens of thousands of people lining the field around the main stage, pennants waving, inflatable toys being thrown in the air. The noise was tremendous. Rhi looked very small, out there on her own. Polly grabbed Ollie's hand and squeezed, hard. She hoped Rhi would be OK.

"Give it up for our prize winner," cried the loudspeaker. "RHI WILLS!"

TWENTY-THREE

Everyone went nuts as Rhi's name boomed out across the field. The pennants flapped hard. The inflatables were thrown a little bit higher.

Rhi cleared her throat. "Thanks," she said shyly. "I'd like to sing you a song I wrote recently. And I'd like to dedicate it to my friends Lila, Polly and Eve. Particularly Eve. I wouldn't even be here if it wasn't for Eve. She made me audition. I don't know where she is right now, but if there's a red-haired girl standing next to you screaming, that's probably her."

The crowd laughed. There was a lump of emotion in Polly's throat as big as a rock.

Rhi strummed the guitar lightly. The sound travelled out into the crowd. "It's about having the strength to be who you really are," she said. "And it's called 'Being Me'."

It was a song Polly had never heard before. She wondered if Rhi had written it after Eve's shock announcement about her sexuality. The words seemed to fit, perfectly.

"Being me," Rhi sang, "is harder than I want it to be, being me is riding out the waves in the sea, being me is harder than a diamond in the ground, but being you doesn't work, I've found."

The crowd was swaying already, waving like seaweed in a wide and brightly coloured ocean.

"Being me," they sang back as Rhi played, "is harder than I want it to be."

Polly felt her eyes filling with tears. The words were so true.

"It's all about yourself, ain't nobody else, there's only one of you before they broke the mould," Rhi sang. "Don't be afraid to fail the grade, you gotta cry before you fly, it's the golden reason why . . . you are you and I am me. . . And that's the truth of it you see. . ."

"Being me," sang the crowd.

"That's the truth of all we see," Rhi sang, putting in a final flourish on the strings, "being me."

And it was over. The crowd went nuts. Whistles and klaxons ripped the air. Arms waved more madly than ever.

"And that was Rhi Wills, a new star in the making!" called the loudspeaker, and the crowd cheered louder than ever.

Polly found that she was jumping around in circles, wrapped tightly in Ollie's arms. The sound of the crowd filled the whole backstage area. They were still cheering.

Rhi appeared at the top of the steps that led down from the stage, breathless, eyes shining.

"You were brilliant!" Polly squealed, pulling her friend into a hug. "Completely wonderful!"

Rhi's eyes looked a little teary as she accepted a hug from Ollie as well. "Thanks, Polly. I couldn't have done it without you. And you know the weirdest thing? Singing that particular song just clarified something really important in my head."

"What? That you're born to be a star?" Ollie enquired. "We could have told you that!"

"That Max isn't the right guy for me," Rhi explained. She still looked a little stunned. "I can see it so clearly now. Singing out there was like hearing my own words for the first time. I'm *not* being me when I'm with him. I just have to find the strength to break up with him." *Him . . . him . . . him. . .*

Rhi's last words had a strange, echoing quality that made Polly frown in confusion. As if . . .

Rhi swung round at the telltale sound of feedback. The blood rushed from her face.

"My mic!" she gasped. "*It's still on!*"

The crowd outside cheered. There were boos too, and catcalls. Rhi ripped the mic from where it was clipped to her top and threw it to the ground like it was a spider.

"Oops," said Ollie, pulling a face.

"Polly, what have I done?" Rhi moaned in horror, staring at the mic on the ground. "The whole of the festival just heard that. Which means . . . which means. . ."

"I just heard it too," said Max in a hard voice.

Polly, Rhi and Ollie whirled round. Max was standing in the stage wings, flanked by Eve, Lila and Josh.

"Oh my gosh!" Rhi croaked. Her hands were on her burning cheeks. "I'm so sorry, Max . . . I didn't want—"

"Didn't want the whole festival to know what a loser you think I am?" Max snarled. "Looks like that backfired on you."

"Max!" Rhi cried as he stormed away.

She burst into tears. Lila and Eve rushed to put their arms around her.

"You did the right thing, Rhi," soothed Eve. "Maybe not in the right way, but. . ."

"But you can't back down now," added Lila, rubbing Rhi's back.

Rhi turned haunted eyes towards Ollie. "Poor Max! Do you think he'll be OK? I never meant him to find out this way."

"It was an accident," Ollie said, steering Polly away. "Max will be fine."

Polly tried to pull away, back towards Rhi. Ollie grabbed her. Was Ollie mad at her for encouraging Rhi to break up with his friend?

"Ollie," she pleaded, unable to meet his gaze. "Rhi needs me. I—"

"I need you too," said Ollie softly. "Why don't you just worry about yourself for a change?"

Polly stared at him for a long, heartfelt moment. Rhi would be fine. She had Eve and Lila. She was going to be happier without Max, everyone knew that. She didn't need to take care of everyone all of the time.

"You're right," she said at last. "I never do what I want to do."

"So no more meddling?" Ollie enquired.

Polly shook her head.

"Finally," he said. "Now all you have to worry about is me."

Polly frowned. "What?"

"Sorry," Ollie laughed, "that didn't come out right. I meant to say, you have nothing to worry about. Let me take care of *you* sometimes. Deal?"

Polly gazed into his blue eyes. "Deal," she said a little faintly.

She slid her hands around his neck and drew him down to her for a passionate kiss. Ollie returned it with so much enthusiasm, Polly found that he had lifted her off the floor.

As she kissed the boy she had dreamed about for so

many years, Polly was dimly aware of Josh and Lila, heads together, talking quietly by the stage wings as Eve held Rhi and let her cry. Josh and Lila were clearly attracted to each other. It was so obvious. If they couldn't see it, well . . . she might have to help them along.

Maybe her meddling days weren't *quite* over yet. . .

LOOK OUT FOR MORE

HEARTSIDE BAY

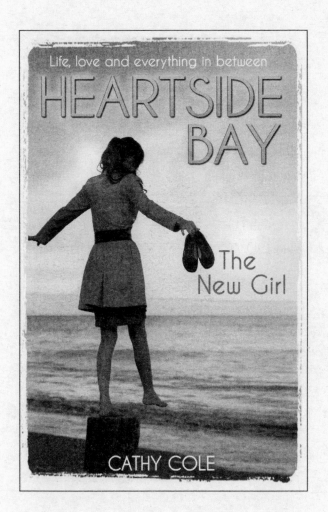

Life, love and everything in between

HEARTSIDE BAY

The New Girl

CATHY COLE

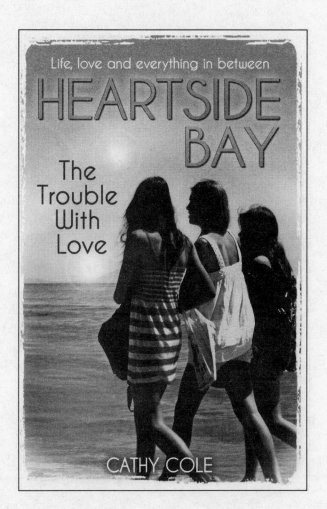

Life, love and everything in between

HEARTSIDE BAY

The
Trouble
With
Love

CATHY COLE

Life, love and everything in between

HEARTSIDE BAY

More
Than a
Love
Song

CATHY COLE

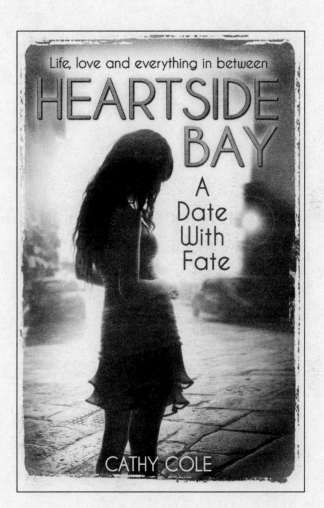

Life, love and everything in between

HEARTSIDE BAY

A Date With Fate

CATHY COLE

Life, love and everything
in between